THE HEALING HEART

THE HEALING HEART

•

BETSY ROGERS

AVALON BOOKS
THOMAS BOUREGY AND COMPANY, INC.
401 LAFAYETTE STREET
NEW YORK, NEW YORK 10003

PRINTED IN THE UNITED STATES OF AMERICA
ON ACID-FREE PAPER
BY HADDON CRAFTSMEN, BLOOMSBURG, PENNSYLVANIA

To my parents-in-law, Roy and Caryl Lundberg, in loving memory. I'm so proud to have known you.

Chapter One

"*Y*ou're the new cannery cook?"

"That's right," said Ashley, wondering at the note of surprise in the speaker's voice. She set down her suitcase in the cluttered office of St. Clair Seafoods and gave the older woman a friendly smile. The latter was seated behind a scarred wooden desk piled high with papers and manila file folders.

"I'm Ashley Martin," she went on. "You must be Mrs. Watkins, the bookkeeper here."

"The bookkeeper, the company store manager—I wear several hats," said the gray-haired woman with a hearty chuckle. "Oh, and just call me Josephine." Leaning back in her swivel chair, she chewed on the stem of her glasses and studied the new arrival.

Ashley felt her smile fade around the edges as she watched the bookkeeper's brow pucker with lines.

"Is something wrong?" she asked self-consciously.

"Sorry for staring," said Josephine with an apologetic wave of her hand. "It's just that there's obviously been a mistake." Her tone was kindly but perplexed.

"Mistake?" echoed Ashley. "I'm afraid I don't understand."

"My dear, we were expecting someone, well, quite a bit older to replace our other cook," explained Josephine. "You're so young; I can't imagine that you've had enough experience for this kind of work. How old are you, anyway?"

"Twenty-five," said Ashley automatically, her mind suddenly in a whirl. The excitement she'd felt upon arriving at the remote Alaskan cannery on Eagle Island was beginning to ebb. This was not at all the reception she'd imagined.

"Well, you look a lot younger," said Josephine, with a little shake of her head. "But that's not your fault, I guess," she added with a smile. She indicated a chair near her desk. "Please sit down. You must be exhausted from your trip. Just put that stuff on the floor."

Ashley removed a stack of file folders from the chair and gratefully lowered herself onto the seat. She'd spent the entire day in a series of airplanes—each one smaller than the last—flying from Seattle, Washington, to that dot of land between Kodiak and the Aleutians, and she was tired, all right.

Only minutes earlier, she'd been looking forward to washing up and changing out of her travel-rumpled blouse and slacks. Now, all thoughts of clean clothes and comfort fled as she focused on the startling discovery that she wasn't what her new employer had expected.

Just then, the cry of gulls and the roar of a seaplane taking off came through an open window.

"Well, there goes your ride back," said Josephine, nodding toward the sound. "The next plane won't be along for another three days—weather permitting, of course," she added. "I guess you're stuck here for at least that long."

"Three days?" said Ashley. She felt her eyes widen as she leaned forward. "But I was hired for the whole summer, until the end of the salmon season."

"Yes, but as I said, we thought you'd be older, more mature," replied Josephine. "You know, someone with a few years of experience under her belt."

"But I have wonderful references," said Ashley.

"Ever worked in a cannery before?"

"Well, no," admitted Ashley.

"For a hundred hungry workers—mainly men—who growl like bears if they aren't fed good food and plenty of it?"

"No, I've never cooked full-time for such a large number of people," said Ashley, feeling a bit daunted by Josephine's kindly but probing questions. "I'm sure I can handle the job, though."

"I doubt that the boss will agree with you," observed Josephine with a rueful smile. "In fact, when he finds out that his Aunt Nora has sent him a cook as young as you, he's going to have a fit." The roll of her eyes toward the ceiling hinted at the wrath of her employer when crossed.

"I'm really sorry," she continued, regarding Ashley with a look of commiseration, "but I can't imagine that Tyler will let you stay on."

"But Nora said that she'd sent Mr. St. Clair word that I was coming," said Ashley. She was feeling more confused by the minute, as well as a little panicky. Were her carefully laid plans and her many preparations for this job going to come to nothing?

Nora St. Clair ran the Seattle offices of St. Clair Seafoods and handled the hiring for her nephew's several Alaskan canneries. Ashley recalled how enthusiastic Nora had been about signing her on as the replacement cook for Eagle Island. Everything had seemed to be falling neatly into place. It now appeared, however, that there had been a miscommunication between Nora and Tyler regarding Ashley's employment. How could such a thing have happened?

"Didn't Nora's fax arrive?" asked Ashley.

"Yes," said Josephine, "I've got it here somewhere."

Burrowing through the mountain of files and ledger books on her desk, she finally extracted a sheet of paper and smoothed out the wrinkles.

"It doesn't tell a whole lot, though," she went on. "Here, judge for yourself." She handed the fax to Ashley.

Ashley read aloud. " 'New cannery cook arriving Tuesday. Excellent references, hardworking, creative. Nora.' " She raised her head and regarded Josephine. "I see what you mean," she said. "It's brief, all right." The complimentary tone of the message pleased her, though.

"Our cooks are always seasoned veterans who've made a career out of cannery cooking," said Josephine as Ashley handed the fax back to her. "Tyler naturally assumed that the replacement would be someone like that." She fixed Ashley with a thoughtful look. "You're a big surprise, believe me."

"Well, I certainly wasn't aware of any of this," said Ashley, giving a wan smile. "Nora told me that as soon as her nephew read my references, he'd be thrilled to have me." She paused, then added with a little frown of concern, ''I had no idea that I was walking into a controversy.''

''Yes, I can see that,'' said Josephine with a sympathetic nod. ''You are rather caught in the middle, aren't you?'' Then she shrugged. ''Nora wouldn't have sent you all this way, though, if she hadn't thought you could handle the work. She's an excellent judge of character.'' Sitting forward, she rested her arms on the desk and laced her fingers together. ''How'd you hear about the job?''

''I met Nora at a garden-club event that I was catering,'' said Ashley. ''I do a bit of freelance catering on the side,'' she added, by way of explanation. ''Anyway, Nora and I got to talking and she happened to mention that she needed to replace the cook at one of her nephew's Alaskan canneries.''

''Yes,'' said Josephine, nodding, ''poor Shorty had to fly home to Ohio rather suddenly. His wife had a stroke, so he'll be looking after her for the next few months.''

''That's a shame,'' said Ashley. After a pause, she continued her story. ''When Nora said that she was frantically searching for a replacement, I told her that I was looking for a summer cooking job and that I'd be happy to go to Alaska.'' She smiled at the memory of the events that followed. ''Nora and I met for lunch the next day to talk it over and she hired me that same afternoon.'' She glanced around. ''It all happened so fast, I can hardly believe I'm here.''

''I can imagine the feeling,'' said Josephine. ''You're a long way from Seattle.''

''Not nearly as far as I'd like to—''

Ashley stopped abruptly, biting her sentence off in midthought. During the awkward little pause that followed, she sharply reminded herself that she'd have to be more careful and guard against such slips of the tongue. Noting the look of curiosity on the bookkeeper's face, she hastened on, anxious to cover her blunder.

"Being away from home won't bother me," she said, fixing a smile on her face. "In fact, I'm looking forward to spending the summer here." She felt her smile fade around the edges. "I'm just sorry to learn that there's apparently been some kind of mix-up."

"Well," said Josephine, with a decisive gesture, "if Nora thinks you're right for the job, that's good enough for me. She's very picky about the people she sends up here.

"Maybe she thought you'd dress the place up a bit," she went on, teasing good humor lighting up her matronly face. "It's been a long time since we've had such an attractive young woman at the cannery."

"I'm sure I wasn't hired for my looks," said Ashley, laughing.

Self-consciously, she tucked a wayward strand of shoulder-length, reddish blond hair behind her ear. As usual, her naturally curly hair was doing exactly what it wanted to, in spite of her efforts to keep it in place with a pair of combs.

"I've worked in some of the best restaurants in Seattle," she added with a little touch of pride.

"Oh, you must have wonderful references," said Josephine. "I only meant that it's a bonus that you're easier to look at than Shorty. I'm sure the crew won't have any objections to Nora's choice."

"Speaking of objections," began Ashley, "maybe I should meet Mr. St. Clair and let him know I'm here." She reached for her purse. "I have a letter of introduction to give to him from his aunt. It should answer any questions he may have about my qualifications."

Josephine compressed her lips and slowly shook her head.

"I wish I could encourage you," she said, "but I think that Tyler's going to be hard to convince. I've worked with him long enough to know that."

"You've been with this company for quite a few years, then?" asked Ashley. She was hoping to pick up a few facts, to better prepare herself for her first meeting with the owner.

"Oh, yes," said Josephine, smiling. "This is a wonderful company to work for. It's been very good to me."

"That's reassuring, at least," said Ashley. She looked around nervously. "Well, I'd better see Mr. St. Clair and get it over with."

"Actually, he's not here right now," said Josephine. She checked the time. "He's out on a tender, picking up some equipment that's overdue. He should be back in a couple of hours." She studied Ashley for a moment.

"I suppose I should warn you," she went on carefully, "that your arrival is a bit ill-timed. Not that it's your fault, of course. You couldn't have known."

"Known what?" said Ashley, with a sinking feeling. Her situation was already discouraging. Was there even more bad news?

"It's no secret around here," said Josephine, absent-mindedly tapping a pen on her desk, "that the cannery's been going through some trouble lately."

"What do you mean?" asked Ashley.

"We've had all sorts of problems," said Josephine, with an ironic twist of her mouth. "It's just been one of those years."

"Losing your cook didn't help," remarked Ashley.

"That's for sure," said Josephine, tossing down her pen. "And Nora sending us such a young replacement just might be the last straw for a man whose nerves are already stretched pretty taut. You might want to remember that when you meet Tyler. He's a wonderful man, and I love working for him. But he's got a lot on his mind these days, and I'm not sure how diplomatic he'll be when he sees you.''

''Thanks for the warning,'' said Ashley, managing a brave smile in spite of the tremulous feeling in the pit of her stomach. ''I hope he'll realize, though, that one of his problems is solved, at least.'' She gestured with her hands. ''He needed a cook, and now he's got a cook. I didn't come all the way up here just to turn tail and run back to Seattle. I accepted this job in good faith and I intend to stay.''

There was a longish silence in the office. The room seemed to echo with the ring of determination in Ashley's voice. As Josephine silently assessed the young woman sitting across from her, a smile spread across her face.

''Yes,'' she finally pronounced, ''I believe you do intend to stay, Ashley Martin. I like your spunk. It's refreshing to find someone who's willing to stand up to Tyler. I think he's going to find you very''—she paused—''interesting.''

She pulled open a drawer, took out a brass ring of keys, and slipped them into her pocket.

''Come on,'' she said briskly, and rose from her chair. ''I'll show you to your room.''

''This is certainly a beautiful part of the world,'' commented Ashley a few minutes later, as she followed Josephine along a boardwalk.

The cannery compound—several white buildings neatly trimmed in blue—nestled against a gentle green slope that was brightly starred with wildflowers. Some low mountains, carpeted in a mosaic of coniferous forest and emerald meadows, rose in the background. Here and there, a stream angled down a cleft toward the sea, like a silver ribbon decorating a velvet cape.

"Yes, Eagle Island is beautiful," agreed Josephine. "It's so wild and dramatic. And it's unspoiled—that's the best part."

"No one lives here?" asked Ashley.

"That's right," said Josephine. "Except for the cannery, the island's uninhabited. You can walk the entire ten miles around it and not see another soul all day." She regarded her young companion. "Is this your first trip to Alaska?"

"Oh, no," said Ashley. "I was born in Anchorage, but I've lived in Washington State for the last twelve years. You see, my mother died when I was thirteen, so my dad sent me to stay with my Aunt Esther in Seattle. Dad was a bush pilot, and I got to come up here every summer to visit him." She smiled with pleasure. "I've never been out to any of the islands before, though. This is really a thrill."

She turned her head to admire the surroundings. Eagle Bay shimmered like a pane of blue stained glass, reflecting the sun and the immense Northern sky that arced over all, as high and airy as a country-market pavilion. Fishing boats rose and fell at anchor amid chattering rafts of gulls, and a fresh breeze blew cool and salty off the water.

The salmon processing plant sat on a dock that jutted out into the bay. Against a faint hum of machinery, Ashley could hear the rattle of a forklift transporting cases of canned fish into a warehouse. Some workers, wearing rubber boots and long white aprons, lounged on the dock, drinking coffee and talking among themselves.

"That's the dining hall," said Josephine, indicating a

building on their left. "You'll probably want to go in there and take a look at the kitchen after you've unpacked."

They walked a few more steps, then Josephine said, "So your dad was an Alaskan bush pilot. My goodness, he must have some exciting stories to tell."

"Yes, he did," said Ashley in a quiet voice tinged with nostalgia. Seeing the questioning look on Josephine's face, she added, "My father died when I was in high school. His plane went down during bad weather."

"Oh, I'm sorry to hear that," said Josephine with a sympathetic dip of her head.

Leaving the boardwalk, they took a grassy path leading to a small cabin standing off by itself.

"You and Tyler have something in common," observed Josephine presently. "Both of his folks are gone, too."

"Oh, really?"

Ashley felt herself stiffen at the mention of Tyler's name. The last few minutes had been so pleasant, she'd all but forgotten her impending meeting with the formidable-sounding cannery owner.

"Yes," said Josephine, talking over her shoulder, "they were killed when a tour bus they were riding in went off the road."

"How awful," said Ashley. "So, Tyler's run the business since then?"

"That's right," said Josephine. "I'm sure it wasn't easy, stepping into his dad's shoes right out of college, but I think he's done a terrific job."

On the cabin's porch, Josephine unlocked the door.

"Shorty bunked in Mitch's room," said Josephine, as the two went inside, "but since you're a woman, I'm putting you in here by yourself."

"Who's Mitch?"

"He's the kitchen helper," explained Josephine. "He's

only seventeen, but he's a good worker, up here to earn money for college. I know you'll like him," she added, smiling.

"Oh, this is charming," said Ashley, setting down her luggage.

"Yes," said Josephine, looking around the room, "this cabin does have a certain something, doesn't it? It used to be Mrs. St. Clair's private little retreat, for sewing or reading." She ran a finger along the top of a bookcase. "Whew, sorry about the dust."

"Oh, that's okay," Ashley quickly assured her. "I'll air the place out and it'll be just fine."

"You'll find clean linens in the bathroom cupboard," said Josephine, then glanced at her watch. "I'd better get back to my books. If you need anything, just let me know. Here's the key." She slipped it off the key ring and set it on a table.

"Dinner was about an hour ago," she added, at the door, "but there's plenty of food left over. Be sure to get something to eat when you go to the dining hall."

"To tell you the truth, I think I'm too nervous to eat a thing," said Ashley, tossing her jacket onto the bed. "I'll probably just have Mitch show me around the kitchen." She hesitated. "I assume that I'll be in charge of breakfast in the morning." It was more of a question than a statement. She wasn't at all sure what her status would be after she'd met Mr. St. Clair.

"That would be my guess," said Josephine. "Even if you're only going to be here for three days, I suppose Tyler will expect you to do the cooking until you leave." She grinned. "But it sounds as if you don't plan to leave." Then her expression sobered. "Say, good luck when you see Tyler this evening. I hope he'll let you stay."

"Thanks," said Ashley.

For the next half-hour, Ashley busied herself in the little cabin. She threw open all the windows to let in the tangy sea air that was wafting up from the bay. Next, she swept the floor, shook out the cheerful rag rugs, and made up the bed.

As she worked, she registered details about the cozy room: an old sewing machine in one corner, shelves crammed with books, a pair of handmade lamps with driftwood bases, colorful throw pillows on a wicker love seat, and a collection of glass fishing floats and pretty seashells.

Ashley's best find, though, was the desk that stood against one wall. With a feeling of pleasure over her discovery, she clicked on the lamp and laid out her notebooks, her Chinese-English dictionary, and her flash cards. Moving an old portable typewriter to one side, she set up her cassette player and language tapes.

She smiled as she surveyed the work space. It was almost too good to be true. What a bonus to find such a perfect place in which to study during her off hours. This was where she'd continue her language lessons in complete peace and quiet.

"He just *has* to let me keep this job," she declared out loud.

Ashley didn't ordinarily believe in omens, but she chose to interpret her finding of the desk as a sign that she'd made the right decision. Accepting this job and coming to Alaska were meant to be, she told herself. This little cabin on an obscure island in the far north would be her haven, her hiding place until fall. Feeling like a wounded animal who had finally found shelter, Ashley knew how disappointed she would be if Tyler sent her home.

Home . . . The irony of the word was like a bitter taste in her mouth. Thinking back to the shattering events of the past few months, Ashley acknowledged that Seattle no longer felt like home to her. She wondered if it ever would again.

Turning her mind away from such thoughts, she stared out the window at a fishing boat that was unloading salmon. She had to admit that she was very apprehensive about meeting the cannery owner. Her show of courage in front of Josephine had been a little act to bolster her resolve. On the inside, she was a mass of quivering nerves. Then she remembered something that seldom failed to calm her.

" 'Never give up,' " she murmured, quoting her beloved grandfather. " 'Follow your dreams, no matter what.' "

Ashley took a deep breath and, feeling better, finished unpacking, transferring her clothing to the dresser drawers and closet.

Carefully, then, she took one remaining item from her luggage and unwrapped the tissue paper from around it. The little Chinese basket had once belonged to her grandfather, John Martin. Of museum quality, it was decorated with antique glass beads and had its own cunning lid that fit perfectly.

Best of all, the basket contained John Martin's World War II diary. Lost for fifty years, the diary had recently fallen into Ashley's hands. Her only regret was that her grandfather had died before its recovery. How pleased he would have been to have it back.

Looking around for just the right spot for the treasured memento, Ashley finally placed it on the nightstand beside her bed. Straightening up, she brushed off her hands and glanced around the clean and tidy room.

"There, that's done," she said with satisfaction.

Her chores completed, it was time to wash up and inspect the cannery kitchen, where she hoped to be working for the next three months. As she was heading toward the bathroom, however, something caught her eye. It was a color snapshot lying on one of the bookshelves.

Feeling a ripple of curiosity, Ashley carried the photo to a window for better light. As she studied the snapshot, she caught her breath. Somehow she knew that the handsome male face staring back at her belonged to none other than Tyler St. Clair.

Ashley guessed that the picture had been taken on Eagle Island when Tyler was about fifteen. He was wearing faded blue jeans, and a T-shirt that stretched across his broad shoulders and already well-muscled chest.

He looked tall for his age, a young man of long limbs and rugged, masculine proportions. There was about him an air of proud independence. Ashley also detected a touch of arrogance in the tilt of his head, and in the rakish smile that played around the corners of his mouth. The expression on his even features suggested that he was well aware of his own masculinity, an aspect that surrounded him like a cloak.

Ashley slowly nodded to herself. The dark-haired teenager with the intense blue eyes and the square jaw must've set female hearts aflutter even at that age. There was a date on the back of the photo. Ashley did a quick calculation; Tyler must be about thirty-two by now.

She put the snapshot back where she'd found it, and discovered that her palms were damp. If Tyler exuded that much confidence as a young man, what must he be like now, almost two decades later? Surely he'd grown accustomed to having others defer to him. It must be rare, indeed, speculated Ashley, when Tyler St. Clair didn't get his own way. Perhaps his early arrogance had evolved, over time, into a cold ruthlessness. Ashley shivered, musing that she'd soon find out for herself.

"Where is she?" roared a deep male voice from just outside the dining hall.

Ashley jumped at the sound, momentarily reminded of an angry bull elephant about to charge an intruder. Since her arrival, two or three hours had passed, during which she'd changed into a light summer dress, met Mitch and discussed the daily meal schedule, toured the kitchen, and planned the menus for the next couple of days.

By that time, dusk had settled over the island and Ashley had the dining hall to herself. She was quietly arranging a bouquet of wildflowers at one of the tables when the man's voice rang out. She looked up and saw a tall male figure looming in the doorway.

Then her heart skipped a beat, for she instantly recognized the adult version of the young man in the snapshot. The intense blue eyes, the thick, dark hair, the smoldering good looks—Tyler grown up was just what she'd imagined, and then some.

Tyler paused and stared over at her, his jet brows lowered in a frown, then he strode forward.

"Ashley Martin?" he brusquely inquired of her.

"That's right," she said, managing to keep the quiver out of her voice.

Her stomach was leaping. Here at last was the moment she'd been dreading since talking with Josephine. Judging from Tyler's impatient tone, and from the stormy expression on his handsome features, Ashley had some fast talking ahead of her if she planned to keep her job.

"You must be Mr. St. Clair," she went on conversationally. She tucked the last flower into the bouquet and forced a friendly smile onto her face. "I've been looking forward to meet—"

"Look, I won't mince words with you, Ashley," broke in Tyler with an impatient gesture. "There's been some kind of mistake. I'm sorry, but I can't let you stay." He raked his fingers through his hair. "When Josephine told me that my aunt had hired someone who's never even worked in a cannery before, I couldn't believe my ears. Nora knows better."

"Mr. St. Clair," began Ashley, wiping her hands on her apron. She took Nora's letter of introduction from her pocket and held it out. "This is from your aunt. It explains why she thought I was the best person for the job."

Tyler ignored the letter. His attention suddenly seemed riveted on Ashley's bouquets. He made a broad gesture toward the bunches of wildflowers on every table, which Ashley had arranged in some empty jars she'd found in one of the pantries.

"What's all this?" he asked, frowning. "What are you doing?"

Ashley laid Nora's letter to one side, but within easy reach of Tyler. His sharp tone made her feel embarrassed and guilty, as if she'd been caught filching coins from the till.

"I was just putting together some bouquets for the tables," she said, with a tentative smile.

"Why?" demanded Tyler.

"Why?" echoed Ashley. The reasons seemed perfectly obvious to her, but she went on to explain nevertheless, wondering at the same time if Tyler always had such a chip on his shoulder.

"I thought some flowers would brighten up the place a bit and make it more cheerful," she said. "If you'll forgive my saying so, the dining hall seems, well, a little drab.''

''Drab?'' said Tyler. His frown deepened as he looked around at the large room with its utilitarian tables and benches, unadorned walls, and curtainless windows.

''The only thing my crew cares about in here is how the food tastes,'' he went on, again piercing Ashley with eyes the color of a fathomless blue sea. ''They couldn't care less about how the dining hall looks.''

''Well, I do,'' said Ashley. Then she could've bitten her tongue. There was a note of challenge in her voice, even though she'd sworn to put on her most diplomatic demeanor with Tyler. So much depended on persuading him to let her stay. Antagonizing him would only hurt her cause.

''What I mean to say,'' she hastened to clarify, ''is that I prefer to work in pleasant surroundings. It's so nice to have flowers to look at, and there're so many of them here. Besides,'' she added in a spurt of boldness, ''these bouquets are a kind of announcement.''

Tyler's brows rose at that. ''An announcement?'' he said in a testy drawl. ''What is that supposed to mean?''

''They say that I'm here now,'' said Ashley. ''When your crew comes in for breakfast tomorrow, they'll know that the new cook has arrived.''

''Little bunches of flowers also scream that the new cook is a greenhorn with nothing better to do with her time than pick posies,'' said Tyler in an argumentative tone. ''Decorating the tables is completely unnecessary.'' He shook his head. ''You've barely set foot off the plane, and you just can't wait to put your stamp on things, is that it?''

Ashley opened her mouth to ask why Tyler was making

such a federal case out of a few flowers. Before she could utter a word, however, he continued.

"What I don't understand," he said aggressively, "is how you had the time to go traipsing out on a flower-gathering expedition. We're shorthanded at the moment, so I'm forced to let you fill in until the next flight back to Kodiak. I'm desperate for help or I wouldn't even consider it.

"So it seems to me," he concluded with heavy sarcasm, "that you should've been familiarizing yourself with the routine around here, instead of practicing your flower-arranging skills."

"Which is exactly what I did," responded Ashley, mustering the last bit of her patience with the abrasive man towering over her. "My expedition, as you call it, took all of ten minutes. And it was conducted only after I'd toured the kitchen and the pantries," she said, ticking the items off on her fingers, "outlined what I expect from my assistant, planned the menus for the next couple of days, and drawn up a preliminary order list for more supplies." She paused to catch her breath.

"From the look of things," she added, "your crew's been living on chipped beef and canned spaghetti. I intend to change that."

"Oh, you do," said Tyler, hooking his thumbs into his back pockets and shifting his weight like a street fighter.

He was wearing a plaid flannel work shirt with the sleeves rolled up over his tanned forearms, and a pair of blue jeans that hugged his long legs. For a moment, he reminded Ashley of a logger who'd prefer to settle their dispute with nothing less than an ax-throwing contest; he fairly bristled with rough-hewn male antagonism. Ashley felt the ground slipping away from beneath her.

"I realize," she said, forging ahead anyway, "that volunteers from your crew have been cooking during the past week. Food out of cans is fine, if that's all one can manage. But you've got a real cook here now, and I intend to put out the very best meals I can." She gestured toward the kitchen. "If you'd like to see my order lists, I'd be happy to—"

"No, no," said Tyler with a dismissive wave of his hand, "I'll check them tomorrow." His eyes restlessly swept over her in shrewd assessment. Then he spoke again.

"You sound pretty efficient for someone so young."

"I don't see how my age has anything to do with it," said Ashley. She paused, then pushed Nora's letter toward him.

"Please," she said, "won't you look at this? Your aunt told me that you'd be glad to have me cook for you once you'd read my references."

"Frankly, I don't care if you've been the head chef at the White House," commented Tyler with dry sarcasm. "Nothing in that letter can make up for the fact that you've had no cannery experience. My aunt was wrong to hire you. I'm sorry that you came up here for nothing, but you're going to have to leave on Friday. And that's the end of it."

"But—"

"Look," interrupted Tyler sharply, "I've had a long, hard day and I'm beat. I've got a cannery to run, and I don't have time to stand around and argue. Face it— you're too young, you've got no background for this kind of job, and it just wouldn't work out.

"I'll have Josephine draw you up a check for two weeks' wages," he continued. "I'll pay for your plane ticket back to Seattle, and we'll just chalk the whole thing up to experience, all right?''

Then, with an air of finality, he turned on his heel and began striding toward the door.

Chapter Two

Swallowing the lump of dismay that had formed in her throat, Ashley grabbed Nora's letter and hurried after Tyler. She caught up with him at the door.

"Please wait," she said.

"What is it now?" he demanded, turning to regard her.

"I'm counting on this job," she said, looking up into his face. "Besides, I . . . I can't go back."

"Why not?" he said with a weary sigh.

He had a tired expression around his eyes, which Ashley hadn't noticed until then. His cheeks and the square outline of his jaw were shadowed with dark beard stubble. Ashley guessed that he hadn't had much sleep lately.

"I said I'd give you two weeks' pay," Tyler went on. "Isn't that adequate until you find another job?" He paused, but not long enough to let Ashley respond. "All right, I'll make it three weeks' pay."

"No, it isn't the money," said Ashley, shaking her head.

"What, then?" said Tyler, rubbing the back of his neck. "Look, talk fast, will you? I still have a lot of work to do tonight."

"I turned my life inside out in order to come up here," she began, remembering the flurry of last-minute details that she'd had to cope with before flying to Alaska.

"Inside out?" asked Tyler. "What's that supposed to mean?" His voice and body language indicated that he was only half listening.

"Well, for one thing," said Ashley, "I sublet my apartment. I'd have nowhere to live if I went back to Seattle now."

"Okay, what else?" asked Tyler, with a barely disguised air of disinterest. Clearly, he didn't give a hoot if she had to roll out a sleeping bag on a street corner.

"I'm letting a friend use my car while I'm gone," continued Ashley. "She has a long commute, her car's unreliable, and, well, I just thought I'd help her out until she can afford to have her own car fixed."

"How very nice of you," commented Tyler.

Ashley noted his dry tone and one mockingly raised eyebrow. Did he think that she was making all of this up? she thought, with growing irritation.

"If I return now," she pressed on, keeping her voice calm and reasonable-sounding, "it'd be unfair to ask for my car back, just when my friend is counting on using it. Don't you see?" she said, lifting her hands from her sides. "Either I don't have a car to use myself, or I leave my friend in the lurch."

Tyler said nothing. Hearing about Ashley's transportation hassles apparently hadn't moved him either. Ashley moistened her lips.

"There's something else," she said, "and in some ways, it's the worst part."

"I just had a feeling it might be," drawled Tyler.

There was the barest hint of a smile tugging at the outer edges of his wide, generous mouth. Ashley couldn't tell, however, if the smile was one of amusement or derision.

"Why do you say that?" she asked with suspicion.

"Because you strike me," he said, briefly dipping his head toward her, "as a woman who saves her big guns for the final volley, that's why." He folded his arms over his broad chest and leaned his long frame against the doorjamb.

"Go ahead," he went on in the tone of someone daring her to swim into shark-infested waters. "Convince me that I should keep you on as my cook because you've made so many . . . sacrifices to come up here."

"I even had to leave Rudy behind," burst out Ashley in frustration.

"Ah, yes," remarked Tyler in a mock tragic voice, "the boyfriend."

Ashley flinched inwardly at the word, yet struggled to maintain an air of composure.

Tyler seemed not to notice her discomfiture. He ran his thumb across the cleft in his chin in an abstracted manner.

"I should think," he continued, "that you'd be over-joyed at the prospect of returning to his waiting arms."

"Oh, for heaven's sake," said Ashley with an impatient little toss of her hair. "Rudy's not a boyfriend. He's my cocker spaniel."

Tyler threw his head back and let out a gust of laughter. The rich, vibrant sound swirled around Ashley like a pesky swarm of gnats that she longed to swat away. Why couldn't the man take her seriously?

"It was hard to go away without Rudy," she said, floundering a bit but determined to make her point. "I left him at my cousin's farm. At least I didn't have to stick him into a boarding kennel, but I already miss him."

"Listen," said Tyler, as the last of his mirth faded, "I'm sorry about your personal problems, but they have nothing to do with me."

"I know that," said Ashley. "The only reason I mentioned any of those things was to impress upon you that I didn't accept this job lightly. I knew that the work wouldn't be easy, and that I'd have to commit myself for the entire summer. It was hard to organize everything at the last minute, but somehow I did it.

"And," she added with feeling, "once I've made a decision, I stick to it." She held up Nora's letter. "The least you can do is read my references and give me a chance to prove myself."

Tyler studied her face closely, his intensely blue eyes narrowed in concentration. Then he expelled a long breath of air, took the letter, and folded it into his shirt pocket.

"I'll read it," he said, "but you're still going to be on that plane on Friday."

"But that isn't fair," said Ashley, her voice rising. "You've judged me before even seeing what I can do."

"Well, I can certainly see what you *can't* do," said Tyler in a withering tone of understatement.

"What do you mean?" said Ashley.

Tyler quickly scanned her from top to toe. A tremor of self-consciousness traveled through Ashley under his bold assessment. At that moment, Tyler reminded her of a cool-headed investor sizing up livestock. The image did little to reassure her.

"How tall are you?" asked Tyler. "About five-five?"

"I'm almost five-seven," said Ashley. She drew herself up a little, once again aware of Tyler's six-foot-plus frame looming over her. "But what does my height have to do with—"

"And you hardly weigh a thing," observed Tyler, his eyes again casually roving up and down her slender figure. "You're going to be cooking for a hundred people. How do you expect to lift heavy pots and pans and bags of produce, hmm? Have you thought about that?"

Ashley allowed herself to smile. "I've got you there," she said, feeling a little spurt of satisfaction. "First of all, I'm actually a lot stronger than I look, and, secondly, Mitch can do the really heavy lifting. That's part of his job, after all, to help out.

"Besides," she continued, "Mitch played football in high school. I just assumed that you'd hired him for his brawn."

"Well, questions of physical strength aside," said Tyler, dismissing the topic with a wave of his hand, "you're still too young and inexperienced. I can't afford to provide on-the-job training to every greenhorn who comes to Alaska. There's too much at stake. I need someone who can step right in and take over."

"I can do that," insisted Ashley. Then an unpleasant thought occurred to her. "Your objections wouldn't have anything to do with my being a woman, would they?"

"Absolutely not," said Tyler. "I don't care what gender you are, as long as you can handle the work and the long, tough hours. We've had female cooks up here before."

"Well, then, why not me?" said Ashley with a shrug.

"Because," said Tyler, using the patient tone of an

adult explaining something elementary to a child, "you are inexperienced and, therefore, unqualified."

"But I still don't see—"

"That is precisely my point," said Tyler with a decisive tilt of his head. "You're so inexperienced, you don't understand what you're getting into. But I do." When he continued, he spoke slowly, emphasizing each word.

"When the season picks up," he said, "and the fish start coming on strong, this place operates virtually around the clock. The work is hard and we get almost no sleep. The cook has to turn out three to four meals a day, plus pastries for the coffee breaks." He leaned toward her. "And you think you're up to that kind of backbreaking grind, day after day?" He paused. "I don't."

"You're just trying to scare me," said Ashley.

"You still don't get it, do you?" he said with a touch of exasperation.

Suddenly, he took her by the arm and began steering her toward the kitchen.

"Where are we going?" asked Ashley, mystified.

"Into one of the back rooms," said Tyler from between tight lips. "There's a mirror in there."

"A mirror?" said Ashley. "But I don't understand—"

"Just come along," said Tyler. "I'll explain when we get there." His fingers felt warm on her upper arm. "Words aren't enough, apparently, so I'm forced to give you a little demonstration."

Tyler crossed the kitchen with Ashley in tow. He hustled her into a pantry that smelled richly of the nutmeg, cinnamon, and other spices that were stored there among bins of flour, sugar, and dry beans. Tyler switched on the light and led Ashley over to a mirror that was mounted on the wall. Then he had her face the mirror while he stood right in back of her.

"Now," he said with the air of a professor who is tutoring a particularly slow student, "tell me what you see."

"I—I don't know what this is all about," said Ashley, a little breathlessly.

She turned her head aside. Tyler pointed back to the mirror.

"Oh, all right," said Ashley in a tone of impatience, "I'm looking."

"And what do you see?" repeated Tyler's deep, masculine voice. His warm breath stirred her hair, whose tendrils framed her face in curly confusion.

Ashley moistened her lips and said under her breath, "This is absurd." Then, catching Tyler's disapproving expression in the mirror, she hurriedly added, "Okay, okay, I see my own face and yours right above it." She shot him a challenging glance. "So?"

"Forget my face," insisted Tyler. "What about yours?"

"What about mine?"

"Describe it, Ashley."

"Two eyes, one nose, one pair of lips," she said, and let out an exasperated sigh.

Their eyes met in the glass. Ashley quickly averted her gaze as she felt a blush suffuse her cheeks. It was most unnerving to be so closely examined.

"It's—it's just a face," she murmured.

"I'll help you," said Tyler. "That face in the mirror—as nice as it is—is the face of inexperience."

"Oh, this is ridicu—"

"Let me finish," he said. "When the going gets tough around here, those eyes of yours will become bloodshot from lack of sleep, you'll start making mistakes out of sheer fatigue, and my crew will eat you alive." He gave a warning rumble deep in his throat. "Cannery workers who don't get fed well can become quite nasty. Then they come griping to me, morale goes down, and I start losing money." He gave a snort of derision. "I can see it all now."

"What can you see?" asked Ashley, the anger building inside her.

"The first week of really hard work around here will be your undoing. Then you'll come to me and beg to be sent home"—he paused—"leaving me high and dry without a cook at the worst possible time."

"I would never do that," said Ashley, her voice tight.

"Well," drawled Tyler, "it's a moot point, isn't it, since you're leaving on Friday, anyway."

Ashley whirled around and faced him.

"You're overreacting," she said with passion. "I'm not a child who can't handle long hours and hard work. Nora described the job to me, and I knew exactly what I was getting into."

"Is that a fact?" said Tyler in a mocking tone.

Then suddenly he leaned against the wall, crossing his arms and giving her an assessing look.

"You're so all-fired sure of yourself," he commented softly, his velvet tones reminding Ashley of a stalking panther. The corners of his mouth lifted, and the depths of his eyes smoldered with interest.

"I just want a chance to prove myself," said Ashley.

She forced herself to look Tyler squarely in the eye. His nearness, however, was making her heart hammer in her chest.

There was a long, potent pause. Then Tyler shook his head and flashed Ashley a smile that revealed his begrudging admiration for her determination.

"Well, I give you credit," he said. "There's one confident woman beneath that attractive exterior. But the fact remains that you're unqualified for this job.''

There was a heavy silence. Then he moved away from her and began walking toward the door.

''The plane leaves at noon on Friday,'' he called back over his shoulder. ''Be on it.''

''Oh—oh, you!'' exploded Ashley after Tyler had left. Obviously, her arguments had meant little to him, for his mind was already made up about her leaving.

Muttering some unladylike remarks under her breath about Tyler, Ashley turned off the lights and headed for her cabin. She was in an absolute fog of frustration. Never in her life had she met a man as stubborn and irritating as Tyler St. Clair.

A shape materialized from the shadows as Ashley stormed up onto her porch. She recognized the shape as Tyler's dog Leo, out on a ramble. Ashley had encountered the golden retriever earlier, when he'd come to the back door of the kitchen for some meat scraps. Later, Ashley had welcomed the friendly dog's company as she picked flowers.

''Hi, there, Leo,'' she said, squatting down to ruffle the soft fur on the dog's neck.

Leo wriggled in greeting, his feathery plume of a tail waving from side to side.

''Is your master always so hard to get along with?'' muttered Ashley. In spite of Josephine's warnings about there being a lot on Tyler's mind just then, Ashley found it difficult to excuse the man's prickly behavior.

Leo sat on his haunches and proffered his right paw. Ashley could hear his contented panting and see his canine grin in the dim light. She laughed softly as she grasped the dog's paw and ''shook hands'' with him. Ashley believed that if Leo could talk, he'd have nothing but praise for Tyler. The cannery owner might be touchy and intractable in his dealings with people, but Ashley suspected that a love of animals might be one of Tyler's weak spots.

"I'll bet he's putty where you're concerned," she said, scratching behind Leo's silky ears.

Petting Leo was taking the edge off of Ashley's anger. She gazed past the dog at the bay, where the lights of several fishing boats cast flickering reflections onto the water. A quarter moon had risen, its cool shape a silver crescent suspended in a purple sky. All was quiet and peaceful on the island, and Ashley found it impossible to hold on to her irritation any longer. How could anyone be upset when surrounded with such an abundance of natural beauty?

Half an hour later, Ashley's thoughts churned as she lay sleepless in the darkened cabin. She desperately wanted to keep her job at the cannery. While it was true that she'd turned her life upside down to come to Eagle Island, she had not shared the full story with Tyler. In fact, her move north involved more than she was willing to reveal, a lot more than simply subletting her apartment and lending out her car.

By accepting the cannery job, Ashley had solved the problem of what to do with her summer. Having taken a leave of absence from her regular job in order to embark on a journey that would not begin until fall, Ashley had been dreading the long summer weeks in Seattle with too much time on her hands—time in which to brood and remember things that she most wanted to forget.

Nora's job offer had come at precisely the right moment. Working in Alaska was perfect, for it provided a chance to escape from the city that held so many unhappy memories. And, judging from Tyler's graphic descriptions of cannery work, Ashley would be kept too busy to dwell on the past. The weeks would fly by. Then, when the salmon season ended, she would begin an adventure that would take her to the other side of the world, where an important task awaited her.

Ashley smiled into the darkness. Receiving her grandfather's diary recently had also been a stroke of good luck, for it had opened doors she didn't even know were there. The timely arrival of the diary in its little Chinese basket had seemed like a message from her dear departed grandfather. He'd always encouraged Ashley to take some risks—maybe even burn a few bridges—in order to achieve success in life. His supportive advice echoed in her memory.

Ashley was determined to convince Tyler to let her stay. Suddenly, an idea occurred to her. Switching on the bedside lamp, she padded across to her recipe cards. She'd already decided what to bake for the next day's midmorning coffee break, but now she had a better plan. Searching through her recipes, she soon found what she was looking for.

She scanned the card. These would be a little more trouble than the frosted sheet cakes she'd originally planned to serve, but the extra labor would be worth it. Sheet cakes were rather unimaginative, after all, and, besides, Ashley didn't mind working harder, especially not when there was so much at stake.

As she read the list of ingredients, a little flame of hope began to burn inside her. If she was going to persuade Tyler to let her stay, it would probably be through her cooking skills. All other considerations aside, that was why she'd been hired in the first place—to cook. Tyler felt that she was unqualified and couldn't handle the job, did he? All right, she'd prove him wrong.

"I'll be the best cook this cannery has ever had,"

vowed Ashley with quiet fervor as she climbed back into bed. Turning over onto her side, she felt a little shiver of excitement just before she dropped off to sleep. She could hardly wait for morning to arrive.

"Where's Mr. St. Clair?" asked Ashley, looking around the dining hall.

Breakfast was nearly over and most of the crew had already returned to work. While Mitch was clearing tables, Ashley had wandered over to where Josephine was sitting alone to make her inquiry.

All during the serving of the meal, Ashley had watched with keen anticipation for Tyler to make an appearance. The thought had occurred to her that after he'd gotten a night's rest and eaten a good breakfast, he might change his mind about her staying without any further arguing on her part.

"Oh, he often skips breakfast," said Josephine, answering Ashley's question as she poured herself another cup of coffee.

"Hmm, I see," said Ashley, sitting down opposite Josephine. She tried not to let her disappointment show.

"He claims it's because he doesn't want to take the time," said the older woman, sipping from her cup, "but I believe I know the real reason."

"What's that?"

"I think he got out of the habit of eating in the morning because he didn't care much for Shorty's food," said Josephine with an amused chuckle. "Shorty was a good basic cook, mind you, but sometimes he got things a little wrong. He couldn't manage decent coffee, for example, so Tyler started brewing his own in his office." She again raised her cup to her lips. "He's going to be sorry he missed your coffee, though. This is excellent."

"Thank you," said Ashley in a distracted manner.

"And these biscuits are divine," rhapsodized Josephine. She broke another one apart and spread it with generous dollops of butter and raspberry jam.

"I'm glad you like them," said Ashley.

They sat in silence for a moment as Josephine finished her biscuit. Then she glanced across the table at her young companion.

"Tyler told me this morning," she said, "that he's sending you out on the next plane. I'm really sorry, honey. I can see how much you want to stay."

Ashley regarded the older woman. "And I mean to do just that," she said with quiet determination. "I'm not on that plane yet. I've still got two more days to prove myself."

"Well, if you keep serving food like this . . ." said Josephine, with a meaningful nod.

"All of the cooking skills in the world won't help, though," said Ashley with a sigh, "if Mr. St. Clair doesn't show up for meals."

She glanced at the door, hoping that Tyler would appear, after all. Just then, he entered the dining hall and headed toward the kitchen.

"Excuse me," said Ashley to Josephine and rose from her seat.

She crossed the room and entered the cooking area.

"Oh, there you are," said Tyler, turning to regard her. "I thought I'd better take a look at those supply lists you mentioned last night."

"Of course," said Ashley, maintaining a steady voice. Her whole body felt primed to resume their battle of wills from the night before, but she intended to keep her wits about her, even though Tyler's presence set her stomach to fluttering.

"They're right over here," she continued in a businesslike tone, brushing past Tyler to reach for some sheets of paper. She handed them to him.

"Thanks," he said with what could have passed for a polite smile.

Ashley watched him with piqued interest as he quickly scanned the lists. He was wearing jeans and a sky blue polo shirt whose shade called attention to the more intense hue of his eyes. A lock of dark hair fell over his forehead and his lips were pressed together in concentration. Was it just Ashley's imagination, or did Tyler really seem less abrasive today than he'd been at their last meeting?

"Okay," he said, nodding, "these look fine. I'll give them to Josephine and have her place the orders." He folded the lists and put them into his pocket.

Just then, Mitch bustled into the kitchen. The sandy-haired teenager was carrying a couple of empty coffee carafes and a stainless-steel tray mounded with soiled cutlery.

"Great biscuits, Ashley," he called out to her with a big grin. "Everyone said so."

"Thanks," said Ashley, warmed by the praise. Then she snapped her fingers as Mitch left the room.

"Oh, that reminds me," she said, thinking out loud. "I want to set some sourdough sponge this morning for pancakes the day after tomorrow." She glanced at Tyler. "It'll take that long to make enough batter for this crowd."

"Shorty left sourdough starter?" asked Tyler, in surprise.

"No," said Ashley, "I brought my own."

"You brought starter with you?" said Tyler, an unmistakable note entering his voice. He was clearly impressed but trying hard not to show it.

"It's been in my family forever," said Ashley with a nonchalant shrug.

"Hmm," murmured Tyler as he studied her.

"I wonder," said Ashley, "if the crew will like sourdough blueberry pancakes." She was actually wondering if Tyler would like them. That is, if he ever deigned to show up for breakfast.

"Are you kidding?" said Tyler, with a short laugh. "They'll love them." Then he seemed to catch himself. He cleared his throat. "A hungry crew will eat just about anything," he added.

"That's not what you said last night," said Ashley, allowing her voice to assume a tone that was partially teasing.

"Maybe you'd better refresh my memory," said Tyler, returning her banter. He leaned back against the counter and crossed his arms over his chest, a posture that defined his well-formed biceps.

"You told me that good food is very important to a cannery crew," said Ashley, rising to his challenge. "If your workers don't eat well, their morale takes a nosedive." She paused. "And low morale can cause you problems." She tilted her head at him. "Perhaps we could say that the well-fed crew is the happy crew."

He studied her for a long moment as a slow smile lifted one side of his mouth.

"Perhaps we could also say," he drawled, "that cannery cooks look kind of cute with flour on their nose."

"W—what?" said Ashley. "Flour on my—"

She lifted a corner of her apron and brushed it across the top of her nose. Momentarily thrown off balance, Ashley felt both strangely warmed by Tyler's comment, as well as unnerved by the sudden change of subject.

Just then, the sound of a loud, hoarse call came from somewhere outside.

"What in the world was that?" asked Ashley with a nervous laugh.

"Come on," said Tyler, taking her arm. "I'll show you."

Out on the back porch, Ashley stared in surprise as, with a flurry of black wings, a large raven landed on the railing. The bird took a couple of hopping steps along the wood, cocked its head, and fixed Ashley with intelligent dark eyes.

Ashley knew that ravens were common in the far north. She'd often seen them when visiting her father, but always at a distance. Never before had one landed a few feet from her, and then proceeded to inspect her as soberly as a police officer.

"Don't be afraid," said Tyler. "It's just Merlin. Sorry if he startled you."

"Is he someone's pet?" asked Ashley, entranced by the beautiful bird with the glossy ebony feathers.

"Merlin's not really a pet," said Tyler. "He's free to come and go as he likes."

"Then why does he seem so tame?" said Ashley. "I've never seen a raven act this trusting before."

"A couple of years ago, I found him on the beach with an injured wing," explained Tyler. "The poor thing was starving and would've died if I hadn't brought him back to the cannery to set his wing and nurse him back to health. As soon as he could fend for himself again, I set him free." He chuckled. "He still drops in to say hello almost every day. I guess he got used to all the attention." He gently stroked Merlin's breast feathers with the back of his fingers. "Didn't you, fella?" he added.

Merlin fluffed out his feathers and blinked his eyes.

"What an interesting story," murmured Ashley as she studied the creature. Learning that Tyler had once taken pity on a helpless, starving raven gave her a glimmer of hope; he couldn't be a complete ogre, could he?

"Oh, I should probably tell you something about Merlin," said Tyler, a twinkle in his eye.

"What's that?"

"He sometimes gets into mischief by taking things."

"What kind of things?"

"Whatever catches his fancy," said Tyler with an indulgent quirk of his lips. "He's especially fond of shiny objects, but it can be anything, so be very careful about what you leave lying around. If Merlin can carry it off, he probably will.

"Yesterday, for example," he continued, "he flew off with somebody's baseball cap. I'm sure he thinks it's some kind of game, because he always brings his booty to me." He laughed. "I always return the stuff, of course, if I can figure out who it belongs to."

"Thanks for the warning," said Ashley with a chuckle.

Just then, a couple of other ravens flew overhead. With a raucous call of greeting, Merlin flew off to join his wild cousins as they winged toward the mountains.

"Don't worry, he'll be back," said Tyler, following Ashley's gaze.

They watched the birds in silence for a moment, then Ashley turned to regard Tyler.

"You know something?" she said, having decided to take a chance and be candid with her employer. "You're much nicer today."

"Yeah, well," said Tyler, rubbing his chin, "that's what a night's sleep will do for a person." He paused, then went on. "Maybe I was a little hard on you last night. Sorry if I hurt your feelings or anything like that."

"No, not at all," said Ashley.

"Now, don't get any ideas," said Tyler.

"Ideas?"

"About this cooking job," he said. "You're still leaving on the next plane out of here." He raised his hand to keep her from arguing. "No way have I changed my mind about that."

"But—"

Tyler glanced at his watch. "Will you look at the time," he said. "Gotta run."

Before Ashley's lips could form a response to Tyler's obvious dodge, the man had disappeared around the corner of the building. A sudden taste of bitterness rose at the back of her throat. She felt foolish and naive for having allowed herself to be lulled by her and Tyler's easy give-and-take of the last few minutes. What a mistake to assume that such pleasantries meant that Tyler had experienced a change of heart. If anything, he seemed more determined than ever to send her home.

Just then, a plan formed in Ashley's mind. She reentered the kitchen and began gathering the items she needed.

"If he thinks that I'm going to give up that easily," she muttered angrily under her breath as she worked, "he's got another thing coming."

A few minutes later, she stepped back to survey the finished results. Adding a creative touch here and there, she picked up the loaded tray and headed for the door.

Feeling a bit like the mountain going to Muhammad, Ashley strode toward Tyler's office, filled with a sense of purpose. Even if Tyler didn't eat one mouthful of the food on the tray, Ashley was determined that he see a sample of the first meal she'd prepared for his crew.

On the way, she encountered Josephine, whom she let peek under the tea towel covering the food.

"Oh, honey," exclaimed Josephine, "that's beautiful."

"It's nice of you to say so," said Ashley. "I just want your boss to see what he's missing by skipping breakfast around here." There was steel in her voice.

The kindly older woman seemed to understand Ashley's plan without any further explanation. She patted Ashley's arm.

"Good luck, honey," she said.

"Thanks," said Ashley, "I suppose I'll need it."

Chapter Three

" "Come in," said a masculine voice in response to Ashley's light knock.

Ashley took a deep breath to steady her nerves. Then she pushed the door open and entered Tyler's office, carrying the cloth-covered tray. She shoved the door closed behind her and regarded the cannery owner.

Tyler was seated behind a large oak desk, his brow creased with concentration as he riffled through a sheaf of papers. His dog Leo was asleep nearby on a little rug.

"Oh, it's you," he said, looking up. "What do you want? If you've come to argue your case again, I'm afraid I'm too busy to listen."

"I've brought you some breakfast," said Ashley, ignoring his brush-off.

She looked around the crowded room with its file cabinets, brass lamps, and framed pictures of sailing ships. "Where would you like this?" she added brightly, indicating the tray.

"You needn't wait on me," said Tyler. "Besides, I rarely eat breakfast."

"Yes, so I've heard," said Ashley. The tray was getting heavy. "But you know what they say about breakfast being the most important meal of the day."

"You're here until Friday to cook," Tyler reminded her, "not fuss over me like a mother hen. Now please take that back to the kitchen."

Instead, Ashley set the tray down on a table near Tyler's desk, carefully disguising her disappointment over his initial rejection.

"Why," she observed, "you haven't even had any coffee."

There was a coffee machine behind Tyler, which obviously hadn't been used that morning. The clear glass pot was dry and empty.

"Hmm, what's that?" Tyler looked up. "Oh, coffee. Uh, no, I didn't take time to make any." He nodded toward the tray. "Does your errand of mercy include coffee?"

"As a matter of fact, it does," said Ashley, ignoring his sardonic tone. She reached for an insulated carafe, which she'd filled from one of the large urns in the dining hall.

"Well, you can leave that, then," said Tyler. Muttering under his breath, he added, "I just hope the stuff's better than Shorty's."

Ashley pretended not to have heard Tyler's last comment. Instead, she poured him a cup of the steaming brew and set it down in front of him. He absentmindedly took a swallow, then he drank again.

"This is good," he said, sounding surprised. He drank some more. "Hmm, very good. Just put it right here where I can reach it."

Ashley felt a little surge of triumph as she moved the carafe closer to him. Now to get him to taste her food.

"Are you sure I can't tempt you with this"? she asked, sliding the tray toward him.

As she lifted the cloth, the savory aroma of warm eggs nestled in a creamy mushroom sauce filled the room. Ashley noticed that Leo stirred in his sleep as the delicious fragrance tickled his keen doggy nose.

Tyler, however, remained irritatingly and steadfastly unmoved. He stared at the tray, which held a beautifully arranged plate of eggs, Canadian bacon, three steaming biscuits, and some fruit compote. Small dishes of butter and raspberry jam completed the picture, which was as pretty as the cover of a cooking magazine.

"You seem to have gone to a lot of extra trouble with that," he finally commented, yet made no attempt to reach for the tray. "But what makes you think that you have to fix special meals for me?" he said, regarding her from beneath lowered brows. "I'm perfectly happy to eat exactly what my crew eats, not some kind of fancy—" He waved his hand toward the tray. "—gourmet food. You have enough to do without cooking two separate menus."

"I wouldn't dream of preparing separate menus," said Ashley, feeling her temper rise over Tyler's display of ungraciousness.

Only then did she realize that, on an unconscious level, she'd taken the tray to Tyler as a kind of peace offering. With this gesture, she hoped to recapture the pleasant tone that had developed between them at the dining hall that morning. Now, she felt sharply let down by Tyler's abrupt refusal to eat her food.

"Do you mean to tell me," said Tyler slowly, "that this is the same meal the crew had this morning?"

"Oh, for heaven's sake," said Ashley, laughing. "You make it sound as if it's something really exotic, like stuffed squab on a silver platter." She shook her head. "It's only eggs baked in a mushroom sauce."

"But it's so different from what the crew usually gets," said Tyler. Ashley couldn't tell if he approved or not.

"Yes, I know," she said in wry understatement. "I found the containers of biscuit mix and the boxes of frozen hash browns that your other cook left behind. No disrespect to him, but processed food just isn't my style."

"Humph," grunted Tyler. "Well," he went on, "the crew can enjoy your different style for two more days, I guess. Just don't get too carried away over there."

"Oh, darn," said Ashley, unable to resist, "I was planning to flambé the luncheon entrée at each table."

Tyler looked sharply at her.

"Just kidding," she said, holding up her hands, palms out.

There was a longish pause as Tyler bent over his work again. Clearly, their conversation was over and Ashley had been dismissed. Instead of turning to leave, however, she stayed put.

"Speaking of two more days," she began, moistening her lips. "Have you read your aunt's letter yet?"

"Hmm?" Tyler looked up. "Oh, Nora's letter. Actually, I haven't had a chance."

"Maybe you're afraid to read it," said Ashley boldly.

"And what is that supposed to mean?" drawled Tyler.

"When you read about my qualifications and background,'' said Ashley, ''you may regret having told me to leave on Friday.''

''You're still hoping that I'll change my mind,'' said Tyler with an air of incredulity.

''Of course,'' said Ashley, raising her chin.

''Well, I'm not going to,'' said Tyler, giving a decisive shake of his head. Then, seeming to relent, he added, ''Oh, all right, sit down. I'll read the letter now.''

He took it out of a drawer as she lowered herself onto the edge of a chair in front of his desk.

''You seem to think,'' Tyler went on, ''that something in this letter will sway me, but I assure you that you're wrong. So we may as well get it over with.''

He unfolded the piece of paper and began to read silently as Ashley watched him and held her breath.

''Hmm,'' he said presently, ''I see here that you've worked at Chez Pauline in Seattle.'' He favored her with a brief glance of approval. ''I've eaten there several times. The food's excellent.'' He continued skimming down the page. ''And you've catered banquets at the downtown convention center.''

''You see,'' interjected Ashley, ''I've cooked for large groups before.''

''But not day after day for weeks on end,'' Tyler pointed out unnecessarily.

''That's true,'' said Ashley, ''but I know I can do it. Hard work doesn't scare me.''

''Just burning up with stamina, are you?'' commented Tyler. ''You wouldn't last a week up here.''

''If that's a challenge,'' said Ashley, sitting forward, ''I accept it.''

Tyler ignored her spirited remark as he continued reading the letter.

''Okay, I'm impressed,'' he said after a while. ''I'll

give you that. Your background's better than I thought, even though you haven't had any cannery experience.'' Then he paused and a slight frown crossed his handsome features.

''Wait a minute, what's this?'' he said. ''It says here that you're a schoolteacher.'' He regarded her with an expression of curiosity.

''That's right,'' said Ashley. ''I've been teaching first grade for three years. All of my cooking jobs were during my summer breaks. The dates are right there beside—''

''Yes, yes, I see them,'' said Tyler.

He tossed the letter onto his desk. Then he gazed over at Ashley, his blue eyes narrowed in concentration and a muscle working in his jaw.

''You're a real mystery,'' he said finally.

''I—I have no idea what you mean,'' said Ashley, feeling a little flustered under his scrutiny.

''Why would someone who can cook at an elegant restaurant like Chez Pauline,'' said Tyler in a measured voice, ''want to fly to a little dot on the map and sling hash all summer at a fish cannery? I don't get it.''

''I beg your pardon,'' said Ashley, bridling. ''Did you say sling hash?''

''Figure of speech,'' said Tyler, waving aside her objection. ''You know what I mean. There's a world of difference between Chez Pauline—where, as I recall, you have to make reservations days in advance—and this place.'' He gave a short burst of dry laughter. ''My workers aren't exactly genteel diners. They're more the rough-and-ready type. So, why did you take this job?''

''It sounded interesting and challenging,'' said Ashley truthfully, ''and I wanted to see this part of Alaska.''

She'd already decided not to mention any other details about her personal circumstances. She didn't know Tyler

well enough, and, in any case, her private life was none
of his business.

"You're not telling me the whole story, are you?" said
Tyler, with a shrewd tilt of his head and the attitude of a
bloodhound who has just whiffed an intriguing scent.
"Come on, Ashley," he added with smooth insistence.
"What's the real reason why you're up here?"

Ashley's stomach fluttered at Tyler's words, and the
sensation that he could read her mind stole over her. Suddenly, she felt like a student with a guilty conscience being grilled by the school principal.

"I just told you," she hedged, determined to brazen it
out. "The job sounded interesting. It came up right as
summer break began, so the timing was perfect, and, well,
here I am."

"I can think of at least one good reason," said Tyler,
"why an attractive young woman would sign on to cook
at an Alaskan cannery."

His insinuating tone caused Ashley's smile to fade.

"You're up here to snag a husband aren't you?" he
said.

Ashley's mouth fell open and she simply stared at him
for a moment, too surprised by his comment to say a word.

"I am *not* up here to 'snag a husband,' as you so col-
orfully put it," she finally said from between tight lips.
"Trust me, that's the last thing on my mind."

"Naturally, you'd deny it," said Tyler with a smugness
that made Ashley itch to slap his face.

"Oh, for two cents," she said, glaring at him, "I'd ask
one of those fishing-boat skippers out there to take me to
Kodiak this instant."

"I'm sure you'd find someone willing to take on a pas-
senger," he remarked blandly. "Go ahead and leave—I
won't stop you."

"I wouldn't give you the satisfaction," snapped Ashley, then added, "You're just goading me on purpose."

"What's that supposed to mean?"

"If you anger me badly enough to make me leave," she continued, "your conscience won't bother you quite so much for not letting me keep this job. You're afraid that I can't take it up here, that I'm not up to the many challenges you've so graphically outlined for me.

"Well, I have news for you, Mr. St. Clair," she went on, leaning toward him to stress her point. "I am here to stay."

"You'll be on that plane on Friday," declared Tyler, sitting forward and bringing his palm down hard on his desk.

Ashley swallowed around the lump that had formed in her throat. Tears of anger and frustration were stinging the corners of her eyes, tears that she refused to shed in Tyler's presence.

Suddenly, inspiration struck. She reached for the untouched plate of food. By then, the eggs had cooled, the lovely cream sauce had congealed, and the biscuits had lost their steamy warmth. Ashley again regarded her antagonist.

"I came over here," she said, her words stabbing through the air at him like angry steel darts, "to make peace with you. I can see that I was wasting my time. I won't make that mistake again. If it's war you want, fine, you've got it.

"And if you won't eat this," she added, indicating the food, "I bet I know who will."

Then she clucked her tongue at Leo, who'd awakened by that time and was sitting up and sniffing the air with interest. Ashley put the plate onto the floor.

"Come here, Leo," she coaxed.

The dog's ears pricked at the sound of his name. He didn't have to be asked twice. Wagging his tail, he walked over to the plate and obligingly began to eat.

Ashley straightened up, brushed off her hands, and regarded Tyler.

"Well," she said, "at least someone appreciates my efforts."

She felt a sudden spurt of perverse satisfaction as she watched Tyler's face darken. Before he could vent his spleen, however, she turned on her heel and left the room, resisting the urge to slam the door behind her.

By the time Ashley reached the kitchen, some of her anger had dissipated. Replacing it, though, was the uneasy feeling that she'd probably gone too far. As gratifying as her final touch of drama had been, she wondered if her show of defiance had provoked Tyler beyond all hope.

With a heavy heart, she began assembling the ingredients for the coffee-break pastry. She'd go ahead and follow her plan to be the best cook the cannery had ever had. She doubted, however, if even a blue-ribbon chef could change Tyler's mind now.

"Ashley!"

A couple of hours had passed. Ashley was working alone during the crew's mid-morning break when Tyler's voice rumbled through the kitchen. Mitch had already taken the trays of pastry and urns of coffee down to the dock, and was busy serving the crew there.

"I'm in here," she called out from the pantry, where she was organizing the spice shelf. Her stomach muscles tightened; Tyler sounded angry.

"So what else is new?" she muttered to herself.

Tyler entered the room and strode over to her. "Cream puffs?" he said without any preliminary remarks.

"I beg your pardon?" said Ashley, looking up in surprise.

"My crew is eating cream puffs down on the dock."

Tyler's mood of antagonism seemed to fill the little room with a palpable presence. He stood with his feet firmly planted and regarded Ashley with eyes that sparked with blue fires of indignation.

"That's right," said Ashley. She had no idea why he was so upset. "It's their coffee break. Did you have a cream puff?" With an air of composure, she returned to her task. "You must be hungry by now," she added mildly.

Then she had to hide an amused smile as the gratifying image of Leo wolfing down the breakfast meant for Tyler flashed into her mind. Perhaps she shouldn't have reminded Tyler of their earlier quarrel, however, for needling him surely wouldn't help her cause. Fortunately, he ignored her reference.

"No, I haven't had a cream puff," he said in a tight voice.

"What is it, then?" asked Ashley in a puzzled tone.

"You're going to spoil my crew," said Tyler, "that's what."

"Spoil your—" Ashley looked at him in bewilderment. "I'm afraid I don't understand what you mean."

"I'll tell you what I mean," began Tyler, stabbing the air with his finger.

Just then, Mitch's head poked through the doorway.

"Hey, Ashley," he called out. Then he saw Tyler. "Oh, sorry, Mr. St. Clair. I didn't mean to interrupt."

"That's all right," said Tyler, nodding toward the teenager. "Go ahead."

Mitch's boyish face creased in a grin. "I just wanted to tell Ashley that her cream puffs are a big hit, that's all," he said. "The workers have already eaten what I took down to them and they're asking for more." He regarded Ashley. "We've still got a couple of trays in the cooler, haven't we?"

"Yes," said Ashley, "go ahead and take them."

She felt a warm glow of pride. How satisfying to learn that her efforts with puff pastry, vanilla cream filling, and powdered sugar had pleased the crew so much.

Mitch turned to leave. Then he paused and spoke to Tyler.

"Should I save you a couple, Mr. St. Clair?" he said. "They're going fast."

"No, thanks, Mitch," said Tyler, his voice sounding a little strained. At that moment, he looked as if he'd rather die than let a cream puff touch his lips.

Once again Ashley had to turn away to hide her amusement. What was there about cream puffs that had Tyler so up in arms?

"Okay," said Mitch, who seemed unaware of his boss's black mood. "Boy, you ought to see it down there, Ashley," he said. "It's like a little party." Then he hurried off.

"See what I mean?" said Tyler in an accusing tone.

"No," said Ashley, "I don't see what you mean at all."

"Didn't you hear what Mitch just said?" he asked, jerking a thumb over his shoulder.

"Well, yes, but—"

"Thanks to you, there's now a party atmosphere down on the dock," he cut in with heavy sarcasm.

"So?" said Ashley, shrugging. "I should think you'd like to see your crew enjoying themselves on their break."

"I do," said Tyler, "but this is carrying things too far."

"What do you mean?"

"You're going to spoil my workers," repeated Tyler.

"They're not used to having cream puffs on their coffee breaks, for crying out loud." He leaned toward her. "What do you think this is, anyway, a resort? Why make something so complicated?"

"You obviously don't know the first thing about pastry," Ashley fired back at him. "Because if you did, you'd know that cream puffs are one of the easiest desserts in the world to make. Puff pastry for the shells is simplicity itself.

"Basically," she continued, ticking the ingredients off on her fingers, "all it takes is butter, eggs, and flour. After the shells are baked, you—"

"Please," said Tyler in the manner of someone who can endure no more. "Spare me the cooking lesson."

"I'll spare you that," said Ashley, "if you'll spare me the lecture."

Ignoring her crisp retort, Tyler continued.

"What happened, anyway?" he said. "Didn't you find Shorty's list?"

His eyes restlessly swept the room, as if the list might magically spring into his hand.

"Shorty," he went on, "had it all written down—what he served on breaks on Monday, what he served on breaks on Tuesday, and so on."

"I found his list," said Ashley.

"Well, then?" demanded Tyler.

"I thought the crew might like a change, that's all," she said. "Having the same thing all the time can get a little old. Nothing against Shorty," she continued, "but he seemed to rely heavily on sugar cookies and cinnamon rolls."

"What's wrong with cinnamon rolls?" barked Tyler.

"Nothing," said Ashley. "As a matter of fact, I plan to serve them myself on Friday, but I make mine out of sourdough. I think they're better than the usual kind, if I say so myself.''

There was increasing tension in the room as Tyler glowered at Ashley, who held her ground. She spoke again.

''What's all this business about spoiling your crew?'' she asked. ''I should think you'd want the best for them. After all, everyone knows that contented employees work better. As we've already discussed,'' she pointedly added.

''They work just fine as it is,'' said Tyler. ''And of course I want the best for them. But don't you see, you're creating a real problem for me. If my crew gets used to food that's a cut above what they usually have, I'll hear nothing but grumbling when you leave on Friday.''

''So that's what this is all about,'' she said. ''You're afraid that they'll like my cooking so much, they'll want me to stay.'' She laughed. ''Well, all the better, then.''

''That's not how I see it,'' snapped Tyler, visibly annoyed by her mirth. ''You're making yourself indispensable, so that I'll be forced to let you stay on.''

''You make me sound devious and underhanded,'' she flared, her anger bubbling to the surface at last. ''I'll make no bones about the fact that I want to keep this job and put out the best food possible. But I'm certainly not trying to manipulate your crew into siding with me. What nonsense.''

''Look,'' said Tyler presently, in a calmer voice, ''just tone it down a little, all right? Serve regular food and everything will be fine.''

''What you mean is mediocre food.''

''Call it what you like,'' said Tyler, giving a dismissive wave of his hand, ''but just do it.''

''I'm afraid that isn't my style,'' she said.

''Then make it your style,'' said Tyler, biting off his words.

"I'm sorry," said Ashley, maintaining her composure, "but I can't agree to that. You're asking me to lower my standards, which I refuse to do." She raised her chin and looked him squarely in the eye. "I work hard and I'm proud of that. You, of all people, must understand what I mean. From what I can see, you work pretty hard yourself."

The room was silent as Tyler stared at her. The expression on his face changed, as if her words had struck an inner chord that he knew by heart. Then he let out an explosive breath of air.

"You . . . are an impossible woman," he said in a tone that was both exasperated and admiring.

"Thank you," she said with a flicker of a smile. "I'll take that as a compliment."

He started toward the door.

"See you at lunch?" she called out in a hopeful voice, but he was already gone.

A few minutes later, Josephine entered the pantry. She popped what was left of a cream puff into her mouth, then brushed the powdered sugar from her lips.

"Ashley," she said, "your cooking is going to be the death of my girlish figure." She laughed good-naturedly and patted her well-upholstered hips. "Those cream puffs were out of this world."

"Thanks," said Ashley. Although she smiled, she sounded drained and cheerless. "I'm glad you liked them."

Josephine regarded her thoughtfully and her manner grew serious.

"What's wrong, honey?" she asked, stepping closer to her young friend.

"Oh, it's that boss of yours," said Ashley, setting down a tin of dry mustard with a hard tap. "I don't seem to be able to please him, no matter what I do. Every time we're together, the sparks just fly.''

''Well, it's been my experience,'' said Josephine, chuckling, ''that sparks always fly when two strong-willed, independent people go head-to-head over a conflict. But I suspect,'' she added, ''that he's intrigued by your drive and determination.''

''Did you say intrigued?'' said Ashley, shooting her a look of skepticism. ''I think he finds me more irritating than intriguing. He even accused me of signing up for this job to find a husband.'' She rolled her eyes. ''That's the last thing on my agenda.''

''You don't ever want to get married?'' gently probed Josephine.

''No,'' was Ashley's immediate response. Then she added, ''That is . . . the subject doesn't interest me right now.'' She looked away, hoping that Josephine would let the topic rest.

''Well,'' said Josephine, ''marriage may not be on your agenda, but I think that the subject's on Tyler's mind these days.''

''Oh, really?'' said Ashley. In spite of her air of disinterest, she noted that her pulse had shot up a notch or two.

''Tyler doesn't confide in me,'' said Josephine, ''so it's just a hunch.'' Checking her watch, she added, ''I'd better get back to my desk. Don't worry, Ashley. You two young people will work things out.''

With a twinkle in her eye to accompany her cryptic remark, Josephine departed.

Chapter Four

Ashley stood in the empty pantry, mulling over Josephine's remarks. The suggestion that Tyler might be intrigued by her, Ashley, seemed preposterous, and yet . . .

She recalled a certain look in his eyes when their glances had met in the mirror the night before. The silence between them had lasted a heartbeat too long, as Tyler's gaze revealed a quickening of interest. Even as he drove home his points about how unqualified Ashley was for the job, his expression retained around the edges that same spark of interest and curiosity.

With a flash of insight, Ashley realized that, had she and Tyler met under other circumstances—different time, different place—they would have been instantly drawn together. Instead, they had encountered each other in a situation that placed them at sharp odds. Tyler's doubts about Ashley's ability to handle the job, and Ashley's determination to hang on to her position, no matter what, had automatically pitted the two of them against each other.

Ashley sighed, remembering how it felt to stand with Tyler and listen to his story about saving Merlin's life. During those few moments, she'd found a chink in Tyler's armor and sensed his appealing vulnerability. As a result, she'd allowed herself to believe that she and Tyler could be on amicable terms, in spite of their conflict. But, she acknowledged now with another little sigh, she saw that she'd been wrong.

It was probably just as well not to become too friendly with Tyler, Ashley admitted ruefully. *Be careful,* she warned herself. *You've been down that road before, and look where it got you.* With that, she returned to her work.

A couple of hours later, Ashley saw Tyler enter the dining hall. The crew had already been served their lunch and were seated at the long tables eating. The pleasant sounds of talking and laughing, interspersed with the clinking of cutlery on china, filled the room.

Tyler put a couple of plates on a tray and hurried over to the steam table. His manner was that of someone rushing into a takeout restaurant.

"Welcome," said Ashley, walking over to help him. "Glad you could make it."

Tyler glanced up sharply at the hint of irony in Ashley's voice.

"I do eat occasionally," he said, returning her sarcasm. He began spooning rice onto the plates.

"One for you and one for Leo?" teased Ashley, taking a chance that Tyler would now see the humor in their morning confrontation.

She was rewarded with a half-smile and a cocked eyebrow.

"Okay," he said in a deep rumble, "you upstaged me royally at breakfast. I guess I had it coming, too." Then he shook his head. "No, this other plate's for Josephine. We have to eat lunch at our desks today, I'm afraid."

"Are you sure you can't stay and eat here?" said Ashley, hiding her disappointment.

"Very sure," replied Tyler. "The chores have really piled up since yesterday. If we work through lunch, I think we'll get on top of things."

He let her ladle some shrimp and savory-smelling sauce over the rice, then he moved on to the steamed broccoli and carrots.

Ashley consoled herself by recalling that half a loaf is better than none. She'd been looking forward to observing Tyler's reaction to her cooking. That he was finally sampling her food was some progress, at least.

Tyler added some knives and forks to the tray.

"Well, that's about it," he said, pulling some paper napkins from a dispenser.

"I'm sorry you're both so busy," said Ashley.

"Some days are just like that," said Tyler, giving a philosophical shrug. With that, he turned and carried the tray from the room.

Later on, Josephine entered the dining hall. By that time, Ashley was rolling out some pastry back in the kitchen. She looked up from her apple dumplings, which were for the afternoon break, then walked over to the steam table.

"Dare I hope," she began with arid humor, "that Mr. St. Clair liked my lunch?"

"He loved it," said Josephine, her eyes twinkling.

"Good!" said Ashley.

"I thought you'd appreciate hearing that," said Josephine with a chuckle. "He wants to see you, by the way."

"Why?"

"I'm not sure."

Ashley hastily brushed off her flour-dusted hands, removed her apron, and told Mitch that she'd be gone for a while.

A couple of minutes later, she was standing alone outside Tyler's office. Before knocking on his door, she paused to compose herself. She was wearing a pair of jeans and a pink cotton shirt, informal attire that was perfectly suited to her job and her rustic surroundings.

Nervously, she brushed her hand across her cheek, which felt enflamed, her temperature rising at the mere thought of being in the same room with Tyler. Not usually so easily ruffled, Ashley found it annoying that this particular man could disturb her so thoroughly.

She tapped on his door.

"Come in," called out a male voice that was, by then, beginning to sound familiar.

When Ashley entered the room, she found Tyler standing at a file cabinet, searching through one of the drawers. He looked up.

"You wanted to see me?" said Ashley.

"Yes," said Tyler.

He strode across the room, then perched on the front edge of his desk, his long legs extended, and regarded Ashley.

"I want to return something that belongs to you," he said, taking a small rectangular object out of his pocket. "At least, I assume it's yours. It has your name on it."

"Where did you find that?" said Ashley, instantly on guard. He was holding up one of her Chinese-language cassette tapes.

"Actually," said Tyler, "I didn't find it. Merlin did."

"Merlin?" Ashley had forgotten about the raven's habit of filching items that didn't belong to him.

"That's right," said Tyler, turning the tape over in his hands. "I heard him calling on the porch. When I went outside, he flew up to my shoulder with this tape in his beak."

"I—must have dropped it yesterday when Josephine was showing me to my cabin," said Ashley. "Thank you," she added, as Tyler handed her the tape. She hastily stuffed it into her pocket.

"So," said Tyler, "why are you learning Chinese?"

"It's none of your business," snapped Ashley.

"Whoa," said Tyler, holding up his hands. "Sorry. I'm just curious. You don't have to jump down my throat."

"No, you're right," said Ashley, reining in her irritation. "I'm sorry. I . . . I just happen to like languages, that's all."

"There's no reason why you're studying Chinese, in particular?" prodded Tyler.

"It's a beautiful language," said Ashley, forcing a nonchalant air about herself, "and I thought, well, I thought that—"

She stopped as she realized that there was probably no harm in Tyler learning part of her story. Moreover, she could tell by the expression on his face that he would not leave the subject alone until she'd satisfied at least some of his natural curiosity.

As if reading her mind, Tyler spoke. "Come on, Ashley," he said. " 'Fess up. Why are you studying Chinese?"

"You make it sound so sinister," said Ashley with a nervous laugh.

She was playing for time, wondering how she could

respond honestly without delving into certain areas that she didn't want to share. When Tyler continued to wait patiently for an answer, though, she was forced to break her silence.

"Oh, all right, I may as well tell you," she said, expelling her breath. "I'm studying Chinese because I'm moving to China in the fall."

"Sorry, but you've lost me," said Tyler. "I thought you had a teaching job in Seattle."

"I did," said Ashley, moistening her lips. "But I've taken a leave of absence so that I can spend the next two years working at an orphanage in Shanghai."

"The next two years?" said Tyler, a thoughtful look crossing his face. "That's a long time." He paused. "But why?"

"It's a complicated story," said Ashley truthfully. "In a nutshell, the orphanage is starting its own school and they need someone to organize their English-language department. They asked me to help them out with that and I agreed. I'll still be teaching—I'll just be in another country, that's all."

"Clear over on the other side of the world," said Tyler.

"That's right," said Ashley. "I'm really looking forward to it."

"I still don't understand," said Tyler. "How did you even hear about such a job?"

"I've been corresponding with the director of the orphanage," said Ashley. "She mentioned the position in a letter."

"Did you go to school together?" asked Tyler. "Is she a friend of yours?"

"No," said Ashley, "I've never met her. She got in touch with our family last winter, because, many years ago, my grandfather had a connection with the orphanage. As I say, it's a long story.''

Studying Tyler's face, Ashley could tell that he was apparently satisfied with the bone she'd thrown him and was ready to let the subject rest. This would be a good time to make her escape. She glanced at her watch.

''I'd better get back to the kitchen,'' she said. ''Thanks again for returning my tape. And don't worry, I won't let my language studies interfere with my work.'' She held her head high. ''Trust me—by the end of the salmon season, you'll be glad you kept me on.''

''You're still hoping that, by some miracle, I'll change my mind.'' His tone had softened a shade. ''Aren't you?''

''Of course,'' said Ashley.

A sudden upwelling of emotion caused her to look down and clasp her hands together. When she raised her head again—mercifully dry-eyed—Tyler was regarding her with a reflective expression on his face.

''You really want this job, don't you?'' he asked.

''I told you I did.''

''Yes, but never exactly why,'' he pursued. ''I get the impression that it's more than just employment to you. And if you're not looking for a husband . . .''

He paused and, like a dog on a scent, fixed her with a penetrating look.

To Ashley's dismay, the conversation was again straying dangerously close to areas of her life that were too private to discuss. Wanting to change the subject, she cast about for ideas and said the first thing that popped into her head.

''I wish you'd eaten lunch in the dining hall,'' she said. ''If you had, you would've seen how much your workers enjoyed the meal.''

"Humph," muttered Tyler, his brow lowering at her remark, which was obviously meant to sway his opinion.

"Admit it, Mr. St. Clair—I can handle this job and you know it."

Without warning, Tyler chuckled deep in his throat as if he were savoring a private joke. Ashley was further surprised when he reached out, caught her by the hand, and pulled her toward him. Because he was still sitting on the edge of his desk, his face was almost on a level with Ashley's. Gazing into his ocean-blue eyes at such close range, Ashley wondered what it was that she saw flickering in their depths besides amusement.

Could it be he actually liked her?

"I'll admit several things," began Tyler with studied leisureliness. His fingers clasped Ashley's in a circle of warmth. "I like a woman who can hold her own. Your lunch was excellent. And . . ." He paused. "I want you to stop addressing me as Mr. St. Clair. Please call me Tyler.

"There's one more thing," he went on in a teasing way.

A slow smile spread across his face, making Ashley think of molten sunshine on a secluded beach. Some potent seconds ticked by.

"I'm really impressed," he finally continued, "by how you get into your work."

"I'm not sure I know what you mean," said Ashley, feeling flustered at being that close to him. The air in the room suddenly seemed warmer, as if a hidden hand had turned up the thermostat.

"You have flour on your face again," he said in a voice that had gone curiously husky. "It's on your cheek this time."

"Mr. St. Clair, I—"

"Tyler," he corrected her with gentle insistence. Then he reached over and brushed the flour from her cheek.

The warmth of his fingers on her skin sent a little tremor through Ashley. It had been so long since anyone had touched her with such tenderness. The room became very still as Tyler's hand lingered and then softly cupped the side of her face. Ashley knew in that moment that Tyler intended to draw her to him and kiss her, a thought that provoked in her an unexpected sense of sweet anticipation, in spite of the warning bell that was clanging at the back of her brain.

Just then, a knock sounded at the door. Ashley and Tyler abruptly pulled away from each other, Ashley with a pounding heart, and Tyler with the air of a man who'd momentarily forgotten himself.

"What is it?" he called out, restlessly pushing off from his desk and standing upright.

Tyler's foreman Bob stepped into the room.

"Have you got a minute, Mr. St. Clair?" he said. Then he noticed Ashley. He smiled and removed his woolen watch cap.

"Oh, hi, there, Ashley," he said. "Don't rush off on my account. This isn't private." He turned back to Tyler. "The crew asked me to come and talk with you," he said.

"Is there a problem?" asked Tyler. He regarded his foreman, all business once again.

For Ashley, the magical spell of a moment before had vanished like a wisp of smoke. As her pulse slowly returned to normal, she noted her twinge of regret that Bob's visit had been so ill-timed. With bemused interest, she reflected on the fact that, in spite of all she'd been through in the last few months, she'd actually wanted Tyler to kiss her. She couldn't explain her reaction, except to admit that the act of Tyler leaning toward her for a kiss had somehow seemed the most natural thing in the world.

"There's no problem, Mr. St. Clair," said Bob, shaking

his head. "In fact, it's just the opposite. You see, the crew wants to thank you for something."

"Oh?"

"It's about Ashley," said Bob, glancing in her direction.

Tyler's expression narrowed as he gave Ashley a sharp look. "What about her?" he said, turning back to his foreman.

"The crew wants to thank you for hiring her," said Bob. "No offense to Shorty, but Ashley's the best cook we've ever had up here." He shifted from one foot to the other. "And, well, we just thought you'd want to know how we feel about it."

When Ashley dared to sneak a glance at Tyler, her fears were confirmed. Bob's praise for her cooking was the last thing Tyler wanted to hear. His smile had faded. In its place was a pair of drawn-together brows, a tightened jaw, and a certain paleness of skin that told of his inner struggle not to reveal his true feelings to his foreman.

"Well," he said, with a touch of bravado, "I'm glad you took the trouble to tell me that, Bob. It was, uh, good of you to let me know how the men feel. Tell them . . . tell them I'm glad they approve, will you?"

"I'll do that, Mr. St. Clair," said the smiling and unsuspecting foreman. Then he made his good-byes and left.

Ashley's emotions warred inside her as a thunderous silence descended on the room. On the one hand, she was satisfied and deeply touched that her efforts were paying off. It made her feel proud to have pleased the crew; their reaction could easily have gone the other way. As a result, Tyler must see that her cooking skills were too valuable, too appreciated, and that replacing her would be a mistake.

And that was where the problem lay. Ashley suspected

that Tyler would feel he'd been backed into a corner. If he sent her out now, his crew would surely protest.

Tyler's voice grated through the silent air. "I was afraid of this," he said, more to himself than to Ashley. He turned to her. "I suppose you expect me to let you keep your job now, after Bob's little speech."

"I honestly don't know what to think," said Ashley, with a helpless gesture. "Naturally, I'm flattered that the crew likes my cooking." She looked him squarely in the eye. "Of course, I'm hoping that their opinion counts for something with you."

"Of course it counts," said Tyler with irritable passion.

Then he strode over to the window, jammed his hands into his pockets, and stared out at the bay for several brooding minutes. The hum of the cannery, mingled with the sound of screaming gulls, punctuated the silence, along with the occasional crackle of a CB radio behind Tyler's desk.

Ashley studied Tyler's broad shoulders, the strong column of his neck, and his well-shaped head with its shock of dark hair. She could almost hear the inner debate that must be waging in his brain.

Then, to her surprise, she felt a stab of sympathy for him. Her instincts told her that Tyler was a lonely man. He made his daily decisions as a leader without help from anyone. There must be times, Ashley mused, when the business of running a cannery empire rested heavily on his shoulders, times when sharing his worries with a compassionate listener could have eased some of his stress. And yet he stood steadfastly by himself.

Before Ashley could pursue that line of thought any further, Tyler turned around and faced her.

"If there's one thing I've learned in business," he said

evenly, "it's when not to buck a trend. You're a good cook and the crew obviously likes your food, so—"

"I can stay?" Ashley took an eager step forward.

"Slow down," said Tyler, holding up his hand. "I didn't say that. What I'm saying is that I'm leaning in that direction, that's all."

"When will I know?" asked Ashley, hardly breathing.

"I'll give you my final decision at dinner tonight."

There was a short pause as Tyler's frown faded away. He walked over to Ashley. Gently taking her by the shoulders, he contemplated her face as if surveying a pleasant landscape that promised diverting possibilities. His eyes swept her features, lingering longest on her lips. He opened his mouth as if to speak, then seemed to mentally shake himself. Reaching behind Ashley, he swung open the door.

"You'd better get back to your pots and pans," he said briskly, giving her a gentle nudge toward the exit. "I'll talk with you at dinner."

For the rest of the day, Ashley's mind kept returning to the same topic: Would Tyler send her packing on Friday, or would he let her keep her job?

As she bustled about the kitchen, another subject clamored for her attention as well. She and Tyler were attracted to each other, a development that neither of them could have anticipated. Tyler St. Clair presented a dangerous mix—rugged good looks, intelligence, business prowess, and a down-to-earth appeal. Ashley would have to watch herself. Being around him was a heady experience, but it was also a little frightening because of its potential power to hurt.

"How well I know," Ashley muttered ruefully under her breath as she went about her chores. "Proceed with caution."

That afternoon, Merlin and Leo made an appearance at the back door. Taking a break, Ashley spent a few peaceful minutes with the animals. She patted the gentle dog on his head and gave him some meat scraps. Then she tore apart a cooled apple dumpling and offered the pieces to Merlin, who'd been watching the proceedings with great interest.

"Come here, you beautiful creature," Ashley murmured to the raven. "I forgive you for carrying my tape to Tyler."

Presently, Merlin gave an excited call and rose into the air. Wondering what had caught his eye, Ashley watched where he flew. She was intrigued to see him glide over to one of the boardwalks, where Tyler had just appeared, and land on Tyler's shoulder. Tyler reached into his breast pocket, took out a little treat of some kind, and fed it to Merlin.

Ashley's heart took a flight of its own at the sight of the strikingly handsome cannery owner. For a moment, as she watched—unobserved and at a distance—she wondered how she could be wary of a man who had such a soft spot in his heart for animals.

Shaking herself out of her reverie, Ashley brushed aside any further thoughts on the matter and headed back to the kitchen.

"So he likes animals," she muttered as she pulled open the screen door. "What does that prove?"

As if in cruel mimicry of the metaphorical gate that had slammed shut in Ashley's mind, the door closed behind her with a sharp, final-sounding smack.

As Ashley supervised the serving of dinner that evening, she tried to keep from glancing in Tyler's direction every few minutes. It pleased her that he'd come to the dining hall to eat with everyone else. He was sitting at a table, engaged in lively conversation with Josephine, Bob, and several others. As far as Ashley could tell, Tyler was enjoying the meal.

She was dying to know what he had decided about her job. During a spurt of optimism that afternoon, she'd washed all of the curtains in her cabin and was planning to iron them that night. Now, with nervous flutterings in her stomach, she wondered if she'd been a little hasty in putting down domestic roots. After all, there was still a chance that she'd be leaving on Friday.

It wasn't until after the dessert had been served that Tyler finally approached Ashley. He asked her to walk up the slope behind the cannery with him, so that he could discuss his decision with her at a spot that overlooked the island.

Ashley was burning with impatience and curiosity. Why couldn't Tyler just tell her there and then and be done with it? Why must she take a hike with him in order to learn whether or not she'd be spending the summer at the cannery?

Something in Tyler's manner, however, told Ashley not to plague him with queries. He must have his reasons, she told herself. So, stifling her questions for the present, she hung up her apron and grabbed a sweater. Then she followed Tyler out to a path behind the cannery and they began to climb.

Chapter Five

Neither Tyler nor Ashley said much during the fifteen
minutes or so it took them to ascend the slope behind the
cannery. The hillside was lush with thigh-high grass that
rustled as they passed by. Wildflowers in delicate shades
of blue and pink and yellow nodded in the fresh breeze
that drifted up from the bay. Here and there, birds fluted
their evening songs, sweet melodies that lingered on the
cooling air.

At last, the path emerged onto level ground. Tyler led
Ashley over to a sheltered spot. A rocky outcropping
formed a natural stone bench backed by several small con-
ifers. They sat down and Tyler made a sweeping gesture
with his arm.

"Take a good look, Ashley," he said, indicating the

scene that spread out before them in all directions. "If this isn't paradise, I don't know what is."

Gazing around her, Ashley felt glad that Tyler had brought her up there. The view was grand and beautiful, a rugged landscape that humbled the observer and defied description by mere mortals. Below them, the cannery compound nestled on the shore. From Ashley and Tyler's perspective, the buildings looked as small and insignificant as models in a miniature town. The island itself was an emerald wonder, whose scalloped gravel beaches fringed the water. The bay and the sea beyond glistened in shades ranging from pale turquoise to deep sapphire, capped with foamy white.

"What's that?" asked Ashley, pointing into the distance.

"The bit of land there?" said Tyler. "That's Tulikof Island. It's about a thirty-minute skiff ride from here."

"Does anyone live on Tulikof?"

"No," said Tyler. "There's an abandoned fishing shack on the beach, but that's about it."

"I think I see smoke coming out of that mountain," said Ashley, shading her eyes.

"That isn't smoke," said Tyler, "it's steam. Tulikof has its own volcano that blows its top every now and then."

"Hmm, how interesting."

"You can't see them today," said Tyler, nodding toward the hazy western horizon, "but the Aleutians are that way." He pointed toward the east. "And Kodiak Island is back there, of course."

"You're right," said Ashley, after a few moments of companionable silence, "this is paradise."

"Wildlife seems to think so, too," said Tyler. "There's

a seal rookery at the other end of the island. Every spring the seals return to have their pups on the beach.''

''I've been wondering how Eagle Island got its name,'' commented Ashley. ''Are there actually eagles here?''

''Oh, yes,'' said Tyler. ''In fact, when I was a kid I found a nest on the cliffs above us.''

''Is it still there?''

''I'm sure it is,'' said Tyler. ''I see the eagles flying over now and then.''

His eyes scaled the gray cliffs that rose above them like the ramparts of a medieval castle. Then he gestured toward a small green knoll below them, off to one side, where Ashley could see a rectangle of white picket fencing.

''My parents are buried there,'' he said matter-of-factly.

''Oh,'' breathed Ashley, ''I didn't know that.'' She regarded him. ''Josephine told me that they died in a bus accident.''

''That's right,'' said Tyler. ''They were touring Arizona at the time. I had them brought back here because, well, this was their favorite place in the world. It just seemed the right thing to do.''

''I'm sure it was,'' murmured Ashley, regarding the stoic outline of his face.

''You're probably wondering,'' said Tyler, ''why I brought you up here.''

He stared off across the ocean, scanning the juncture where the sky met the water. Ashley was reminded of a king surveying his domain.

''I love this island,'' he went on, ''this . . . hunk of rock out in the middle of nowhere. I love everything about it—the wildness, the remoteness, the peace and quiet.'' He looked at Ashley. ''If I ever lost it, I think it would just about kill me.''

Ashley wondered at his sudden passion. Was he in danger of losing his cannery and the island with it? It didn't seem possible, and yet she'd already heard from Josephine that the season had gotten off to a bad start. Maybe things were even worse than Ashley had thought.

"The reason I brought you up here," said Tyler in sober tones, "was to impress upon you that I'm responsible for all this." He nodded down toward the cannery. "Whatever happens on Eagle Island is my business. And if something goes wrong, it's my concern." He made a decisive motion with his hand. "I can't afford to let things get out of control. I run a tight ship, Ashley." He looked at her. "Do you know what I'm saying?"

"I'm not sure," said Ashley carefully.

"I find myself between a rock and a hard place, where you're concerned," said Tyler. "On the one hand, I agree with my crew that you're an excellent cook. They obviously want you to remain here." He paused. "So I've decided to go along with that."

"Oh!" said Ashley with a happy little cry. "Thank you. You won't be sorry, I promise."

"I'm already sorry," said Tyler, arching one eyebrow in an expression that aptly conveyed his misgivings. "I'm going against my better judgment, remember. Please be clear about that from the start." He was silent for a moment.

"If you recall," he went on, "I warned you that, when the fish really start coming in, we'll all have to work virtually around the clock to get them processed. You've never done this kind of work before, so you don't know about the horribly long hours you'll put in, with few breaks and very little rest. And that can go on for days at a time. You'll get so tired, you'll practically fall asleep standing up. Your back and legs will ache, and you'll curse me for letting you stay on."

"No, I won't," said Ashley. "I'm not afraid of hard work."

"Yes, well, we'll see about that," said Tyler with a wry glance in her direction. "My concern is that you really don't understand what you're getting into." He sighed, his brow furrowed. "So, I'll let you keep your job on one condition."

"Which is?" asked Ashley.

"That you commit to the whole season," said Tyler. "I can't afford to have you quit when the going gets tough." He turned to probe her eyes with his. "Is it a deal?"

Ashley regarded Tyler, who'd restlessly stood up and stepped a few paces away from her. His solitary figure was framed by a dramatic combination of sky, clouds, and roiling sea. It was an image that reminded her of a princely falcon on a wild and rocky crag.

As she studied Tyler and his surroundings, Ashley realized in a flash of primal recognition that, at the end of the fishing season, she'd be sorry to leave wild and beautiful Eagle Island.

"Yes," she said, from the bottom of her heart, "of course, it's a deal." She paused. "I would never quit suddenly and leave an employer in the lurch." She lifted her chin. "You can count on me."

"Humph," muttered Tyler, piercing her with a look that revealed his doubts. "All right, then," he said, sitting beside her again, "that's settled. Just don't come complaining to me later on."

"You don't have to worry about that," said Ashley. "I wouldn't do anything to jeopardize my summer up here."

"You say that with such passion," he said, laughing briefly. "Why, you'd think that signing on for one of the hardest jobs in the world was some kind of dream come true.''

''The timing was perfect; that's all I mean.''

''Hmm,'' said Tyler thoughtfully, ''there's that subject again. I get the impression that you fought so hard to stay on here because of something other than the job of cooking. Perfect timing, you say?''

''That's right,'' said Ashley, whose hands had begun to fidget in her lap. ''I needed a summer job and your aunt offered me one. End of story.''

''But with your qualifications and background,'' said Tyler, ''you could've easily picked up some temporary work in Seattle.''

''I didn't want to,'' said Ashley, a sensation of uneasiness beginning to spread through her.

''Didn't want to?'' said Tyler, sounding puzzled. Then he added, ''Oh, I get it. You didn't want to be in Seattle.''

''You could put it that way,'' said Ashley. She glanced around. ''It's getting kind of late. Don't you think we should be starting back?''

''We've got time,'' said Tyler smoothly. ''Relax.''

''How can I relax,'' said Ashley, trying to disguise the strained quality that had crept into her voice, ''with you grilling me like this?''

''I'm sorry,'' said Tyler. ''It's just that I want to get to know you better, that's all.'' He paused. ''You're certainly an exception. Seattle's a popular place. Most people want to go there, not escape from it.''

''Who said I'm escaping from anything?''

''You did,'' said Tyler. ''At least, you implied as much.''

''No, I didn't.''

''Sure you did,'' he insisted. ''You told me that you didn't want to be in Seattle.''

"Well, yes," admitted Ashley, "but—but that's not the same as escaping." She passed a nervous hand across her brow. "You're putting the wrong spin on things."

"Am I?" asked Tyler softly. "So why are you trembling, all of a sudden?"

"Please don't say any more," said Ashley, appalled at the sound of her voice, which had thickened with suppressed emotion. Her body was betraying her, giving too much away.

"Hey, what's going on, Ashley?" said Tyler, moving closer and taking her hand. "Are you in some kind of trouble? Is it money?"

"No, no," said Ashley, shaking her head. "It's nothing like that."

"What, then?" said Tyler. "Maybe I can help."

"It's really not your concern," said Ashley, feeling as defensive as a cornered animal. "Anyway, it's nothing that'll affect my work, if that's what you're worried about."

"I'm worried about you," said Tyler sincerely.

"You don't even know me," said Ashley, feeling a quick sting of unshed tears at the back of her eyes.

"That's true," said Tyler and squeezed her hand. "But I already like you." A few silent moments ticked by. "It's a man, isn't it? You're running away from a man."

"Why do you say that?" said Ashley, blinking the moisture from her eyes. She was determined not to shed any more tears over that subject.

"Shot in the dark," said Tyler, shrugging. "Plus there's this." He pointed to the ring finger on her left hand, where a pale, untanned circle showed where a ring used to be.

"Well," said Ashley in a rueful tone, "you're a regular Sherlock Holmes, aren't you?"

"You've either been married," said Tyler, ignoring her jibe, "or engaged. Now, for whatever reason, you're not."

"All right," said Ashley, sighing, "I was engaged and now I'm not." She lanced an impatient look at him. "Nice work, Detective."

"Are you still in love with the guy?"

"No." Her response was firm, final, and absolutely truthful. "I never want to see him again as long as I live," she added, gazing out to sea. "Why do you care, anyway?"

"I like to take a personal interest in my employees," said Tyler. "In the past, I didn't pay enough attention to what was going on with the people who work with me, and, well . . . let's just say that I've learned from my mistakes.

"I'm sorry if I've offended you in some way," he added gently. "This is obviously a very sensitive topic for you. I can see that you've really been hurt." He paused. "The guy must've been a real jerk, though. How anyone could mistreat someone like you is beyond me."

His words, as sincere as any she'd ever heard, caressed Ashley's ears like a warm and welcome breeze after a violent storm. Some hidden, protected part of her heart—sheathed in the armor plate of mistrust—suddenly constricted with longing. When was the last time a man had expressed genuine concern for her?

Just as quickly as this insight came to Ashley, the gates of her vulnerability once again slammed shut. She abruptly pulled her hand away and stood up.

"Since I'll be spending the summer here," she said, steering Tyler toward a completely different subject, "I'd be interested in seeing how the fish are processed."

"I'll take you on a tour of the cannery sometime," said Tyler as he also rose to his feet.

"Thank you," said Ashley. "I'd like that."

She turned to leave, but stopped when she felt Tyler's hand on her arm.

"You're a good cook, Ashley," he said. "I'm glad you're here."

Ashley detected something in Tyler's manner that went beyond an appreciation of her culinary skills. His sea-blue eyes held hers for a long moment, and the air pulsed with an undercurrent of deeper meaning.

When the silence became awkward, Ashley gathered her sweater around her and began stepping toward the path.

"Well," she said briskly, "I'd better get back to the dining hall. I need to start my pastry for the morning coffee break tomorrow."

They started down the path with Tyler in the lead. In the dimming light, Ashley suddenly stubbed her toe and lost her balance. She gave a startled little cry as she pitched forward.

Tyler turned to see what the problem was just in time to catch Ashley in his arms.

"What a klutz," said Ashley, embarrassed. "I tripped on something . . . sorry."

"No need to apologize," said Tyler. "It's getting hard to see out here."

Ashley looked up into Tyler's face, where dusky shadows had settled on his cheeks and brow. His handsome features were framed by his dark hair, which was lightly stirring in the sea breeze. Tyler's unflinching eyes probed hers. She noticed with a quickening of her heartbeat that he was drawing her near and encircling her more firmly in his arms. Although she'd regained her balance, he showed no indication of releasing her. In fact, his hold on her was becoming an embrace.

Ashley caught her breath as the flats of her hands registered the nubby texture of Tyler's wool shirt. As the warmth of his chest beneath the fabric reached her palms, she felt a sudden jolt of longing that amazed her.

Tyler pulled her closer still, using his strong arms to encircle her. She leaned against the solid bulk of his chest. One of his hands splayed at her back, bending her closer to him.

Seemingly of their own accord, or as if in a dream, Ashley's arms went up around Tyler's neck. Her fingers laced themselves in his hair as a ragged sigh escaped her throat. Tyler's lips were near. Ashley could feel his warm breath on her skin.

"You are one tempting woman," murmured Tyler, whose voice had deepened and grown husky. He dipped closer. "So beautiful, so sweet." With that, he lowered his face to hers and claimed his kiss.

Ashley closed her eyes and accepted Tyler's kiss. He began lightly, gently, his lips warmly teasing hers. Then, as Ashley responded in kind, Tyler's embrace intensified.

A rush of emotion, of joy, coursed through her veins as she reveled in the sensation of Tyler's lips on hers. She felt utterly swept away by his kiss, one that combined a sweet tenderness with the spice of something more. Never before had she been kissed like that.

When at last their lips broke free of each other, Ashley opened her eyes and gazed up in wonder at the man towering over her. Her cheeks felt hot and flushed, her legs weak beneath her.

"We shouldn't be doing this," she said.

"Oh, I think we should," said Tyler, laughing deep in his throat.

"No, really," said Ashley, pulling away.

"Hey, what's wrong?" said Tyler, gently drawing her back.

"Oh . . . it's nothing," hedged Ashley, not wishing to delve any further into her private feelings. We've already done too much of that for one night, thank you very much, she thought.

Tyler continued to hold her loosely in his arms. His breath rasped from his throat in ragged sighs. Slowly he shook his head from side to side.

"Mercy, woman," he said, "what are you doing to me?" Then he traced Ashley's lower lip with his thumb. "Kisses like that can really get to a guy." He took a deep, steadying breath and glanced around. "It's late. We'd better walk back to the cannery before it gets any darker." Taking her hand, he began leading Ashley down the path.

A few minutes later, they arrived behind the dining hall, where Tyler kissed Ashley again, lightly this time.

"Now, get in there and start your pastry," he said with a smile. "I'll see you in the morning." With that, he melted into the darkness.

The rest of the week passed quickly as the work pace at the cannery began to pick up. As the days went by, Ashley settled into a busy but pleasant routine. Turning out three meals a day, plus big trays of pastries for two coffee breaks, kept her occupied.

Each night, after retiring to her cabin, she'd listen to her language tapes, repeating the words and phrases until they sounded just right. It pleased her to be making progress with her Chinese. By the time she arrived in Shanghai in the fall, she'd be able to carry on some rudimentary conversations.

As the salmon season progressed, a constant stream of boats came and went in the busy harbor. Ashley saw little of Tyler during the day, except at meals. Now and then, she caught a glimpse of him, down on the dock, striding along one of the boardwalks, or conferring with Bob or Josephine.

The hours right after dinner were different, though, for the pace let up and everyone, including Tyler, took time to unwind and have a little fun. As the days went by, Ashley found herself looking forward to the after-dinner sessions, for she enjoyed the atmosphere of relaxed camaraderie that settled over the cannery as the sun slid toward dusk. She joined in on card games at one of the dining-room tables, usually while keeping an eye on dough that was rising for morning rolls. One evening, she soundly beat Tyler at cards, then laughed until she had tears in her eyes when he told a hilarious story featuring a poor loser.

Once in a while, she'd look up from her work in the kitchen, or from her hand of cards, to find Tyler's eyes on her. At such moments, the noise and bustle of the room would melt away, leaving Ashley with the sensation that she and Tyler were in a secret little world of their own.

Feeling flustered at thinking such thoughts, Ashley would turn her gaze away and silently chide herself. How could she imagine that Tyler was sending her messages with his eyes? Such notions were absurd. And besides, she reminded herself, she wasn't interested.

During this time, she sought safety in numbers and avoided being alone with Tyler. To her relief, he seemed to sense her wishes and appeared content to follow her lead. In the group settings, with their friendly banter and easy give-and-take, she and Tyler, Ashley realized, were getting to know each other. She was grateful when he didn't try to push their relationship any further, but was aware that she always looked forward to seeing him. Although happy to be on such friendly terms, she wanted to avoid anything more complicated.

And yet . . . she couldn't help but remember that she and Tyler had discovered a special chemistry between them, one that had bubbled to the surface—quick and hard to ignore—shortly after Ashley had arrived. It was impossible not to recall the delicious feeling of his arms around her, and the warmth and tenderness of his kisses. Sometimes the memory was so vivid, she had to stop whatever she was doing and close her eyes. Willing the images out of her head sometimes worked, but they always returned. It was most distracting.

One afternoon, there was a stir at the cannery when an unscheduled flight arrived at the island. A sleek chartered seaplane landed in the harbor and taxied up onto the beach. Ashley happened to be standing outside at the time. She shaded her eyes and watched as three men stepped from the plane. They looked around as if coolly taking stock of the place.

Something in the men's demeanor disturbed Ashley, and she wondered about the purpose of their trip. Later on, at lunch, Tyler and the three men sat apart from everyone else and seemed to be deep in discussion. At one point, Tyler frowned and shook his head at one of the visitors, who seemed to be trying to reason with him.

It was with a sense of relief that Ashley watched the three men depart that evening. As their plane roared across the bay for takeoff, it narrowly missed a raft of seabirds, who arose on panicked wings and fled in all directions. Although the men were leaving, their disturbing presence seemed to linger. It was as if they'd left a noxious fog in their wake.

Unable to contain her curiosity any longer, Ashley put

her chores aside and sought out Tyler. She finally found him sitting alone on the beach, out of sight of the cannery.

"Mind if I join you?" asked Ashley, with a tentative smile.

"No, I guess not," said Tyler, returning his gaze to the far horizon.

His less-than-enthusiastic greeting disappointed Ashley, but she told herself that it was probably due to the fact that he had a lot on his mind. It was obvious that he was worried about something.

"Pardon me for being nosy," she said as she sat beside him, "but who were those three men who visited you today?"

"Developers from Seattle, that's who," said Tyler, his voice grating with disapproval.

"Developers?" said Ashley, mystified. "What would they be doing here?"

"They want Eagle Island," said Tyler, biting off his words.

"What do you mean?"

"They want to buy the island and turn it into a resort."

"You're kidding," said Ashley, almost laughing.

"I wish I were," said Tyler, a spark of anger igniting in his eyes. "They want to tear down the cannery and build a hunting lodge. Then," he went on, regarding her, "they're going to ship in big-game animals and fly people up here to shoot them." He paused. "For fun."

"But—but that's an ugly idea," said Ashley, hardly believing her ears. "Shooting animals for fun . . . I've always hated that sort of thing. It's obscene." She looked at Tyler. "Besides, the island would be ruined if that happened."

"Of course it would," said Tyler. He shook his head. "Think of it—hordes of the pampered rich swarming all over the island, shooting everything that moves.'' He formed a fist with one hand and brought it down onto his knee. "It would break my heart to turn this place over to people who don't appreciate it for what it is.''

"Well, those three are wasting their time," commented Ashley, gesturing with her hands. "You love Eagle Island. You'd never sell it.''

Tyler expelled his breath in a long sigh. The planes of his face were etched with worry.

"I'd never want to," he said in a weary voice, "but I may find it hard to avoid.''

"What do you mean?''

"It's a long story," said Tyler, rubbing his eyes. He suddenly seemed very tired.

"I have time," said Ashley, quietly laying her hand on his arm.

Tyler covered her hand with his and gave it a grateful squeeze. He seemed to welcome a chance to talk.

"It's no secret," he said, taking a deep breath, "that this cannery is in financial trouble. The problem actually started a few years ago. Back then, Josephine ran the company store and someone else—a guy named Larry—did the books.

"To make a long story short," he continued, "Larry had been embezzling money from the company. When I finally caught him—last summer, to be exact—he'd run the cannery deeply into the red.''

"How awful," said Ashley.

"Larry was a compulsive gambler," said Tyler. "That's why he was stealing from us, to cover his gambling debts. He owed so much money, his life was in a complete shambles. I was going to press charges, but, in the end, I didn't have the heart to bring the guy down even farther.

"Larry had no way of paying back what he'd stolen," explained Tyler, "and throwing him into prison wasn't the answer, either." He shrugged. "I figured there was no point in trying to punish the guy. Plus, Larry's wife and daughter would've suffered, too, and they'd already done enough of that.

"So, instead," he continued, "I got him to agree to go into counseling and perform some community service, in exchange for not being sent to prison."

"That was very humane of you," said Ashley, mulling over Tyler's story.

"Well, it was realistic, too," said Tyler. "All I would've gained by prosecuting Larry was revenge."

"How does the trouble with Larry tie in with those developers?" asked Ashley.

"I tried to keep the whole mess quiet," said Tyler, "but you know how people talk. I'm not sure exactly how those Seattle guys heard about my financial trouble. All I know is that when they got a whiff of it, they contacted me with an offer. That was a couple of months ago and they've been pestering me about it ever since. Today they told me that they've hired some attorneys to help them flesh out the deal, as they put it."

"Isn't there some way you can save your cannery?"

"One or two good seasons could put us into the black," said Tyler. "In the meantime, my other canneries up in Bristol Bay—which are doing well, incidentally—are supporting this one. If we have a couple of bad seasons in a row, or if some of the big fishing outfits start selling somewhere else, well, that could be the end of Eagle Island.

"If everything goes well," he continued, "—and that's a very big if—I'd like to expand this place. You know, add another processing line and maybe build a second warehouse." He tossed a pebble into the water. "But that's really a long shot, at this point. From the looks of it, I'll be lucky to hang on to the cannery just the way it is."

"You're not in this business only for the money, are you?" said Ashley softly. "It's a way of life for you." She paused, wondering how deeply she should delve into Tyler's personal feelings. "You really love this place."

"Uh-huh," said Tyler, with a catch in his voice. He cleared his throat.

"This has always been my home," he went on. "Selling Eagle Island would be like . . . well, like selling my soul."

He expelled his breath in a rush of air that seemed to rip from the very core of his being.

"But I have to be practical," he continued, "as painful as that might be. If things get much tighter, I'll be forced to sell. I just hope it doesn't come to that."

Just then, as Tyler's woes settled over Ashley like a mournful gray cloud, the nesting bald eagles that he'd told her about soared overhead. They cast dark, thrillingly wild shapes against the sky, which was, by then, awash in the brilliant colors of sunset.

It was the first time that Ashley had seen the eagles. A quick sting of tears sprang into her eyes at the moving sight of the beautiful creatures, such powerful symbols of dignity and freedom. What would happen to the eagles, the seal rookery, and the other natural wonders on the island if developers moved in? It didn't bear thinking about.

"Is there anything I can do to help?" she asked, turning to regard Tyler.

She couldn't imagine how she could assist Tyler, but she nevertheless felt compelled to offer. Something deep inside of her wanted to stand shoulder to shoulder with him on this issue.

"I doubt it," he said, "but it's good of you to ask." He gave a sudden burst of bitter laughter. "Believe me, I won't go down without a fight. I owe that much to—" He stopped.

"Yes?" said Ashley. "You owe it to the memory of your parents?"

"Yes, that," he said, "but also to—" Then he took a deep breath and continued. "Oh, you may as well hear all the messy details."

"What do you mean?" asked Ashley. A feeling of uneasiness stole over her. What was Tyler alluding to?

"The cannery's financial problems," said Tyler, "are a bit more complicated than just embezzled money."

"In what way?"

Tyler laced his fingers through hers and drew her closer to him, as if seeking her warmth and reassurance.

Ashley squeezed his hand in return as she searched his eyes and found there a measure of pain that she'd not noticed before. Tyler's burdens were obviously greater than she'd first thought.

Although she believed him capable of overcoming whatever challenges life dealt him, she could see that meeting those challenges had taken its toll. Tyler had paid heavily in his battles with life's adversities, and Ashley's heart went out to him.

"What is it you want to tell me?" she asked softly.

His eyes held her gaze.

"I'm raising a child, Ashley."

Chapter Six

There was a stunned silence as Ashley tried to digest what Tyler had just told her. She could hardly believe her ears.

He was raising a child?

"I—I didn't know that you'd been married," she said, finding her voice at last.

"No, no," said Tyler, shaking his head, "I've never been married."

"But you have a child?" prompted Ashley.

"I'm not actually Elf's biological father," said Tyler.

"Elf?"

"Her real name's Katherine," said Tyler, a sudden affectionate grin lighting up his face, "but we've always called her Elf. She was such a tiny thing when she was born.'' He glanced at Ashley. ''I can see you're confused. Maybe I'd better back up.''

''Please.''

''Here's where the story gets complicated,'' said Tyler. ''Larry—the guy who embezzled money from the cannery—was married to my cousin Marla. Elf was their little girl.'' He looked at Ashley. ''Are you with me, so far?''

''Yes,'' said Ashley, ''but I don't understand why you're raising their daughter. I mean, you didn't prosecute Larry, so I assume that he's not in prison. And even if he were, Elf would still have her mother. Why isn't Marla raising her?''

''That's just it,'' said Tyler. ''Elf doesn't have her mother. She doesn't have either one of her parents.''

''Why not?''

Ashley was thoroughly confused by that time, so Tyler told her the rest of the tragic story. Soon after being caught for stealing money from the cannery, Larry suffered a massive heart attack. He managed to hang on for a while, but then he died, leaving behind a young wife and a little girl.

A week after burying Larry, his wife was killed in a car accident. She died at the scene. Larry and Marla's little daughter was thus left an orphan. Elf's situation was made even worse by the fact that there were no living grandparents to step in and take her parents' place.

''So that's the whole, sad story,'' said Tyler in a bleak voice. ''Both parents dead within a week of each other.'' His expression darkened. ''Elf was left all alone.''

''Oh, how horrible,'' said Ashley, her voice breaking. She reached up and wiped some tears from her eyes. ''That poor little girl.''

''That's how I felt about it, too,'' said Tyler, offering Ashley his handkerchief. ''Elf had been through so much pain and turmoil, I was determined to somehow make it up to her, so I decided to adopt her and raise her myself. The fact that she's a blood relation made the legalities fairly simple.

"I feel I owe that little girl," he added. "I know it's silly, but I can't help but feel responsible. Larry had that heart attack shortly after I caught him embezzling."

"You mustn't blame yourself," said Ashley. "It certainly wasn't your fault. In fact, you were incredibly understanding with him. You wouldn't even press charges."

"I know, I know," said Tyler with the weary air of having been over that ground many times before, "but I'll always wonder." He regarded her. "Maybe now you see why I like to get to know my employees. After Larry and Marla died, I vowed to pay better attention to the people around me.

"I can't ever replace Elf's parents," he continued, "but I can be a father to her. I love her very much, just as if she were my own child."

"How old is she?" asked Ashley, drying the last of her tears, then handing Tyler's handkerchief back to him.

"Seven," said Tyler.

"Oh, I love that age," said Ashley, smiling.

"You'll get to meet Elf," he said, turning to her.

"Really?"

"Yes," said Tyler, "she's arriving tomorrow. Josephine has a spare room, so Elf will bunk with her. That way, Josephine can help me keep an eye on her, too."

"Where's Elf now?"

"With some Seattle friends of mine," said Tyler.

"I'll look forward to meeting her," said Ashley sincerely.

"Considering what she's been through," said Tyler, "it's a wonder she's not more emotionally damaged than she is. She's just now beginning to come out of all that. I guess kids are pretty resilient. She's recently started calling me Daddy,'' he added, a warm smile lighting up his face. ''That's a good sign.''

Ashley and Tyler sat in silence for the next few minutes. By that time, the sun had dipped low to the horizon and purple shadows had lengthened on the beach. The water in the bay was a deep cobalt blue, dotted here and there with rafts of gray-and-white gulls. Little waves lapped at the shore, each one creating gentle liquid notes as it rose and fell.

Suddenly, Ashley shivered.

''Cold?'' asked Tyler.

''A little.''

''Here,'' he said, taking off his jacket, ''take this.''

He draped the garment over Ashley's shoulders. Gratefully, she gathered it around her and then shivered again, but not from the cold this time. The jacket was warm from Tyler's body and redolent with his scent, one that combined a hint of spicy after-shave underscored by a headier note that was pure male. Ashley closed her eyes for a moment and breathed in the intoxicating fragrance.

''What are you thinking about?'' said Tyler, his face close to hers.

''You,'' said Ashley, saying the first thing that popped into her head. Then she felt her cheeks grow warm.

''That is, I . . .'' Her voice trailed off. ''You smell good.''

''Well,'' said Tyler, dipping even closer, ''I like the way you smell, too.''

He lowered his eyelids and lightly sniffed the air near her. At that moment, he reminded Ashley of a wine connoisseur savoring the bouquet of a tantalizingly complex vintage.

"Ah, yes," he said, a teasing note entering his voice, "I believe I detect Eau de Vanilla Bean with just a hint of Toujours La Spicy Meatball."

Reduced to giggles, Ashley fell back onto the sand.

"Oh," she finally gasped, struggling to sit up again, "I needed that. But I'm getting sand all over your jacket."

"Never mind," said Tyler. "It doesn't matter."

Tyler stretched out beside her and propped himself up on one elbow. He studied her face. Some wayward tendrils of her hair blew across her cheek. Tyler reached over and softly brushed them back, his warm fingers lingering on her skin. He sat up and leaned toward her.

"Jokes aside," he said in a voice that vibrated near her ear, "you do smell wonderful." He lowered his face toward hers. "Do you know what you smell like, Ashley?"

"No," she said, suddenly breathless.

"You smell clean and sweet," murmured Tyler.

He ran his fingers along the curve of her jaw and down the column of her neck.

"It's very appealing," he continued. "If I could bottle that scent, I'd make a fortune. And you know what?"

"What?"

Ashley's voice was a whisper. The air around her and Tyler crackled with tension, as she felt herself being drawn into the depths of Tyler's gaze.

He slipped his arm around her waist. "At the moment, it's driving me crazy."

With that, he lowered his lips to hers. His kiss was long and leisurely, a studied performance that made Ashley feel weak and dizzy. Without stopping to think about it, she twined her arms around Tyler's neck and pulled him closer to her. Even amid the natural beauty all around them, they clung to each other as if the rest of the world had ceased to exist.

"What am I *doing?*" Ashley suddenly murmured against Tyler's lips. She groaned and pulled away from him.

As they both sat up, the magical mood evaporated.

"What is it?" said Tyler, putting his hand on her arm. "Ashley, what's wrong?"

"It's hard to explain," she said, staring out at the water.

"Tell me something," said Tyler. "Why do you always seem to pull away from me whenever I kiss you?" He gave her arm a teasing little shake. "Am I that repulsive?"

"Of course not," she said, laughing briefly. *Anything but,* she silently added, acknowledging the hammering of her heart.

"Then what is it?" he said, putting his arm around her shoulders and nuzzling the soft hairs that curled at her temple.

When she didn't answer right away, he went on.

"Okay," he said in a conversational tone, "we don't have to discuss that right now, if you don't want to. We'll discuss something else. Let's pick a different topic." He paused. "I know—let's talk about cards."

"Cards?" said Ashley in a puzzled voice.

"You know, card games," he said. "I'll tell you a little secret—I can't stand them. In fact, I hate cards."

"What are you talking about?" said Ashley, mystified. "If you hate card games, why on earth do you show up every night in the dining hall to play them?" She laughed. "I thought you were hooked on cards."

"Oh, I'm hooked, all right," he said, cupping her chin in the warmth of his palm and gazing into her eyes. "But it's not on cards. It's on you."

"Please," said Ashley, feeling herself draw back, "you don't know what you're saying."

"Oh, yes, I do," said Tyler. "And don't think I haven't

noticed that you've been dodging me all week. It's been impossible to have a private word with you, because I can never find you alone. You've made sure of that.'' He traced a gentle finger down her cheek.

''When I noticed that you were showing up for those games,'' he continued, ''I suddenly got this strange passion for cards.'' There was a twinkle in his eye. ''I figured it was my only way of getting to spend some time with you.'' He chuckled. ''I almost gave myself away, though.''

''What do you mean?''

''Remember when you beat me the other night?'' he said.

''Yes.''

''Well,'' said Tyler, ''I have a little confession to make. You beat me fair and square, but it was partly my own fault. You see, I sort of lost track of what game we were playing.''

''You're kidding,'' said Ashley, regarding him with amused disbelief.

''No, I'm not,'' said Tyler. ''Right in the middle of a hand, I forgot what we were playing and threw away my best cards.'' He chuckled at the memory. ''As a result, you trounced me good.''

Ashley laughed, it was so funny. ''How could you forget what game we were playing?'' she said.

''You need to ask?'' said Tyler softly, his voice husky around the edges. ''There I am, sitting across the table from a delectable peach of a woman, and you wonder why I can't keep my mind on a silly card game?''

''Tyler, don't—''

''You are so incredibly distracting,'' said Tyler, overriding her protest. ''I can't keep my eyes off you. I love watching you shuffle and cut the deck. You have such graceful hands and such lovely, slender wrists.''

So saying, he raised one of her wrists to his lips and planted a soft kiss on its sensitive inner surface, where Ashley's pulse warmly leapt.

Tyler continued itemizing her charms.

''And then,'' he said, ''there's the way you hold your cards up to your face like a fan every now and then, and peer over them with those witchy green eyes of yours. It just about drives me crazy.''

''Tyler, please stop all this,'' said Ashley, ducking her head. ''You're embarrassing me.''

''Don't be embarrassed,'' said Tyler. ''You can't help being so attractive.'' He paused. ''I've been drawn to you since the day you got here.''

''You were quick enough to want to send me straight back, though,'' she reminded him.

''Oh, don't be fooled by that,'' said Tyler with a throaty laugh. ''That was purely a business decision, because I thought you weren't suited to the work. If you'd left, I'd have figured out how to see you again, believe me.''

There was a short silence, which Tyler eventually broke.

''This past week,'' he said, ''has been torture for me.''

''What do you mean?''

''I can't get you out of my head,'' said Tyler, his voice low and urgent. ''It's impossible to concentrate on my work, because thoughts of you keep getting in the way.'' He gave a short, sardonic laugh. ''I have another confession to make.''

''Which is?''

''I invent excuses to swing by the dining hall during the day,'' he said, ''just to catch a glimpse of you. Whenever I'm around you, I try not to stare, but I may as well tell myself not to breathe." He kissed her cheek. "Sweet Ashley," he murmured against her skin, "you're driving me out of my mind.

"I couldn't sleep last night," he went on, "so I went out for a walk. I noticed that your light was still on, so I started up toward your cabin. I was going to ask if you'd like to step outside and look at the sky with me. It was a beautiful night. There was a full moon."

"Yes, I know," said Ashley. She remembered the moon's cool, pale light pouring through her open window like liquid silver.

"Just as I got to your cabin, though," said Tyler, "your lights went out. I didn't want to disturb you, so I turned around and left without knocking." He took her hand. "Correct me if I'm wrong, Ashley, but I got the distinct impression that you saw me coming and turned off your lights to avoid talking to me."

Her silence was his answer. It was true; she had glimpsed him coming up the path and had hastily doused the lights and scurried into bed. Her heart pounding, she'd heard his footfalls on the porch, sensed his hesitation at her door, and then finally listened to him step away into the night.

"Why, Ashley?" he asked. "Why did you do that? Have I offended you in some way? Please tell me. I've got to know."

"Tyler," said Ashley, turning to gaze into his face, "you're a very nice man and I like you. You haven't done a thing to offend me." She hesitated. "It's just that, well, I don't want to get involved with anyone. That's why I don't think it's a good idea for us to be alone or for you to be kissing me. Please try to understand."

"But I don't understand," said Tyler. "Why do you

have such an aversion to romance?'' He paused. ''Does it have something to do with this?''

He touched her left hand, indicating the pale circle on her finger, the ghost of an engagement ring.

''Yes,'' she admitted, her voice barely above a whisper.

''The guy must've really hurt you,'' said Tyler. ''Can you tell me about it? Did you break up with him, or was it the other way around?''

''He broke off the engagement,'' said Ashley, trying not to show any emotion.

''He must've been nuts,'' said Tyler with feeling. ''When did it happen?''

''A few months ago,'' said Ashley, her eyes staring out at the distant horizon. ''Last December. Right before . . . right before our wedding.''

''You were planning a Christmas wedding?'' asked Tyler.

''Yes.''

''So what happened?''

''I don't want to talk about it,'' said Ashley abruptly, as she shook her head from side to side.

There was a long, heavy silence, during which Ashley could feel Tyler studying her profile.

''Well, okay,'' he finally said, expelling his breath with a hint of frustration. Clearly, he wanted to hear the whole story, but was apparently willing to let Ashley reveal it to him, or not, in her own way.

''So,'' he continued, ''welcome to the human race.''

''What do you mean?'' asked Ashley.

''Haven't you heard,'' said Tyler, ''that there's no life without pain? Everyone has disappointments. Are you going to let a broken engagement wreck your whole life?''

''No, of course not,'' said Ashley, a defensive note creeping into her voice.

"Then why should it affect you and me?" said Tyler. "You've already told me that you don't love the guy anymore, so what's the deal? Is it just too soon or what?"

Making no reply, Ashley drew up her knees and wrapped her arms around her legs. Then, to her dismay, her eyes overflowed with moisture and tears began running down her cheeks. She buried her face on her knees as a sob escaped from her throat.

"Oh, no," said Tyler in distress, "now look what I've done."

He reached his arms around her in a huge embrace, as if trying to shield her body from blows.

"Please don't cry, Ashley," he whispered urgently. "I'm so sorry. I should've kept my mouth shut. Oh, please don't cry."

He rocked her gently in his arms and presently her crying stopped. Loosening his hold on her, he reached into his pocket.

"Maybe I should just hang on to this," she joked through her tears, as she accepted his handkerchief. "I seem to have leaky eyes tonight." She dried the dampness from her cheeks and blew her nose.

"I feel like a heel," said Tyler with remorse. "I shouldn't have pestered you about it. Ashley, I'm so sorry I made you cry."

"Oh, it isn't your fault," said Ashley sincerely. "Really it isn't. That whole business is still very painful for me, that's all."

"I hate to see you cry," said Tyler, smoothing some hair away from her face. "I much prefer seeing you laugh, the way you did the other night."

"You were hilarious," said Ashley, smiling over the memory of Tyler's funny story. "And now that I know that you didn't even remember what game we were playing, oh—'' She gave a short peal of laughter. ''—it's even funnier.''

They were silent for the next few minutes, sitting side by side as Ashley further composed herself. By that time, darkness had fallen and stars were twinkling in the sky overhead in a brilliant display of celestial bodies. A night bird called from somewhere out on the water, where the ruffled edges of undulating waves reflected the starlight.

''Look,'' said Tyler softly, ''here comes the moon.''

He and Ashley watched as the giant silver disk peeped over the watery horizon. As it climbed into the heavens, it cast a molten patch of illumination across the bay, a magical footpath that drew the eye and transported the senses.

''Oh,'' breathed Ashley, ''how beautiful.''

''Yes,'' murmured Tyler, but Ashley was aware that he was looking at her and not at the moon.

''It's late,'' she said. ''I'd better get back to the kitchen. I still have some things to do tonight.''

They both got to their feet and brushed the sand from their clothes.

''I just want to say one more thing,'' said Tyler. ''Life is short, Ashley. Don't waste your time the way I have. Don't dwell on past hurts, for example. You've got to get on with your life.''

''That's good advice,'' she said carefully. ''Thank you.'' She hesitated. ''But do you really think you've wasted time?''

''Oh, yeah,'' he said with conviction. ''I didn't even know it until I adopted Elf. Raising a child gives you a perspective you never had before. Children tend to, well, center you, I guess you could say.'' He gave a short, rueful laugh. ''My friends who have kids have been telling me this for years, but I guess I had to find it out for myself.

"Anyway," he continued, "it all sort of hit me one morning when I looked in the mirror and realized something."

"What was that?" said Ashley.

"That I was almost thirty-three years old," said Tyler, "and that life was moving on." He shook his head at the memory. "I honestly couldn't see what my life had amounted to, up to that point." He gave a thoughtful pause. "But Elf changed all that. Taking on the responsibility of raising that little girl made me stop and take stock, as they say." He rubbed his chin. "I've got some major holes in my life, Ashley."

"What do you mean?"

"I mean," said Tyler, "that I feel as if I've just been marking time, instead of experiencing—really experiencing—life. Oh, my life's been good, over the years, but when Elf came along, I realized that there are better things out there."

He gave a long, introspective pause as he gazed at the silvery path of the moon on the water.

"I want those things, Ashley," he said with quiet fervor. "I want them soon."

"What do you want?" Her voice was barely a whisper.

"I want a wife," he said matter-of-factly. "I want a wife for me and a mother for Elf. She needs a mother, Ashley, and I need a wife. I'm tired of going through life by myself. I want to settle down and make a home with someone. I'm ready."

Ashley was speechless in the face of such an impassioned declaration. There was no doubt of Tyler's sincerity, and she was almost moved to tears by the sound of urgent longing in his voice.

"Tyler, I—" She stopped. What could she possibly say to him?

"There's something else," said Tyler. "I was an only child, but I want Elf to grow up with a little brother or sister. I'd like to make that happen for her." He chuckled in the dark. "But first I need to find a wife."

A sudden chilly wind blew across the beach. Ashley began to tremble.

"What's wrong?" said Tyler, grasping her arms. "You're shaking all over."

"I'm just—just cold, I guess," she said.

She ducked her head to hide her emotions. The sweet scenario that Tyler had painted filled her with a sense of such loss and yearning, her stomach knotted with pain. If Tyler only knew how impossible such a plan would ever be for her. With all her heart, she certainly wished him well, however.

Stepping away from him, she began walking up the beach toward the kitchen. He fell in beside her.

"I hope you find what you're looking for," she said. "It sounds like a wonderful plan."

"Hey," he said, halting her progress through the sand by taking her arm, "am I not making myself clear enough here or what?"

"What do you mean?"

"Well," he said, raking his fingers through his hair, "I had this crazy idea that maybe you and Elf and I—"

"No," said Ashley, shaking her head. "No, Tyler."

She tried to pull away from him, but he held on fast. Bringing his face close to hers, he willed her to look into his eyes. By the light of the moon, Ashley could see blue fires of determination burning in his gaze.

"Ashley," he said, "listen to me."

"What you're suggesting is out of the question," said Ashley.

"Relax," he said, obviously trying to calm her. "I have

a habit of saying what's on my mind, that's all. I didn't mean to upset you.''

She became still then, except for the painful slamming of her heart against her rib cage.

"Okay," he said, "all right. Maybe I'm going too fast for you. Im sorry." He paused. "But I just have this—I don't know—this gut feeling that the three of us . . ."

"Stop it!" cried Ashley, clapping her hands over her ears. "I don't want to hear any more of this."

With that, she turned away from him and began escaping up the beach toward the lights of the dining hall.

"Ashley, wait!"

Whirling around, she took off Tyler's jacket and deftly tossed it into his arms.

"Thanks for letting me wear that," she said. "And by the way, aren't you forgetting one tiny little detail?"

"What's that?"

"I already have an agenda, Tyler," she said. "I'm leaving the country in the fall. I'm spending the next two years in China, remember?"

"Maybe I can talk you out of that."

"No, I'm afraid you can't. Now good night."

With that, she fled up the beach and headed for the kitchen, where, with any luck at all, she'd find some blessed forgetfulness among the tools of her trade.

Chapter Seven

The next morning seemed to mock Ashley's dark mood, for the dawn arrived clear and breathtakingly lovely. As she walked from her cabin to the dining hall, she paused, as she often did, to gaze at her beautiful surroundings. The early morning air blew fresh and cool, its fragrance tangy from the sea. Fishing boats bobbed at anchor, and the volcano on Tulikof Island steamed in the distance.

Heavy dew blanketed everything, bending the grass blades over with clear droplets that reflected the sun's rays like a myriad of tiny gems. A nimbus of clouds hid the top of the cliffs behind the cannery. Ashley pictured the eagles' aerie up there, safe and unmolested.

As she resumed her walk, trying to compose herself, Ashley felt a weight settle over her. Even the natural wonders of Eagle Island could not erase the conflicting emotions that clung to her from the night before. Her heart ached when she remembered Tyler's tender, passionate embraces down on the beach, as well as his touching candor regarding his desire for a wife and family. How wonderful it would be to cast aside all of her reservations and yield to the instinctual attraction that she felt toward him.

If only life were that simple, she reminded herself.

Squaring her shoulders, she entered the kitchen, determined to put all thoughts of Tyler out of her mind.

Later on, as the crew was filing into the dining hall for breakfast, Ashley stole a moment from her work and glanced out the window. In spite of herself, she'd been looking for Tyler all morning.

Holding the curtain aside, she felt her heart leap as she spotted him. He'd just descended the stairway that led to his apartment. He paused on the boardwalk and looked around, seeming to admire the beauty of the new day, then he began walking in the direction of the dining hall.

Ashley returned to her work. She kept one eye on the door, though, all the while chastising herself for caring one way or the other if Tyler showed up for breakfast.

About twenty minutes went by, during which Ashley heard the sounds of a seaplane landing and then taking off again. When Tyler still hadn't arrived, she began to wonder what had happened to him. Trying to suppress her curiosity, she began refilling the serving containers in the steam table. Then, for the hundredth time, she glanced across the room, willing Tyler to walk through the door.

At last she saw him.

The large metal serving spoon that Ashley was holding slipped from her grasp and went clattering into a stainless-steel pan. The unexpected noise caused heads to turn in her direction, but only briefly. A buzz of interest rippled through the dining hall as every person present fastened curious eyes on Tyler and the strangely dressed little girl standing beside him.

Ashley realized with a start that the child had to be Tyler's adopted daughter, Elf. What with one thing and another, she'd forgotten that Elf was due to arrive that day. The plane she'd heard earlier must've brought her.

Ashley had the sudden impression that events were moving too swiftly for her. She'd barely learned that Tyler was raising a child, and now, with no time to digest that surprising news, she was going to meet Elf in person.

Ashley watched as the seven-year-old clung to Tyler's hand and glanced shyly around the room. She had large blue eyes, an intelligent face, and wisps of blond hair peeking out from under the cap of her costume.

As if dressed up for a Halloween party, Elf was wearing an outfit that covered her from head to toe in green fabric. The getup included a tail and a row of stand-up scales that marched down her back.

Just the thing to wear on a plane, Ashley chuckled to herself with amusement.

As Elf and Tyler approached the serving area, Ashley hastily tidied her appearance by wiping her hands on her apron and tucking some stray tendrils of hair behind her ear.

"Good morning, Ashley," said Tyler. Thankfully, there was nothing in his demeanor that hinted at their candid discussion on the beach the previous night. "We have a visitor," he added.

"So I see," said Ashley, smiling as she inclined her head toward the child. "This must be Elf."

"Yes, it is," said Tyler.

"How did you know my name?" said Elf to Ashley. She still clung to Tyler's hand.

"Your daddy told me all about you," said Ashley, glancing at Tyler.

"This is Ashley Martin," said Tyler, speaking to the girl. Then he regarded Ashley. "Is it all right if Elf calls you by your first name?"

"Of course," said Ashley.

There was a brief pause as Ashley's eyes met Tyler's. A look quickly passed between them, telling Ashley that Tyler was hiding his emotions for his daughter's sake. A glimmer of interest in his eyes revealed, however, that he fully intended to pursue last night's topics with Ashley another time.

Ashley again regarded the little girl, seeking safer ground among the rituals of courtesy.

"I'm very happy to meet you, Elf," she said warmly. "And I love your outfit. I'll bet you're the first person who's ever flown in an airplane dressed as a dragon."

Elf looked down at her feet and spoke so softly, Ashley couldn't hear her.

"I'm sorry?" said Ashley. "What did you say?"

"I'm not a dragon," said Elf, raising her head.

The expression on Elf's face was so serious for a child of such tender years that, under different circumstances, Ashley would've been tempted to find it comical. Her instincts told her, however, that she had just made her first faux pas with the little girl.

"Oh," she said, "excuse me."

She looked to Tyler for some kind of clue.

"Tell her what you are, sweetheart," said Tyler, gently coaxing the child.

"I'm a dinosaur," said Elf with a touching note of pride in her voice.

"Oh, yes, of course," said Ashley. "Now I see." She smiled. "Well, you're a very elegant one, I must say."

"Thank you," said Elf. Then she added, "I'm going to be a dinosaur scientist when I grow up."

"What a good idea," said Ashley.

She noticed that the child had not smiled once, and she wondered if Elf was always that sober. Then she remembered the sad events of Elf's past and her heart squeezed with compassion for her.

Tyler spoke.

"The family she's been staying with made the costume for her," he explained to Ashley. "Then Elf, here, talked them into letting her wear it on the plane," he added with an indulgent chuckle.

"Where's Shorty?" asked Elf, looking up at Tyler. "I want to show it to him."

"Well, sweetheart," said Tyler, "I'm afraid Shorty's not here this summer."

"Why not?" asked Elf. Her eyes grew large as a quizzical expression crossed her face.

"His wife needs Shorty to stay home and take care of her for a while." He pulled Elf closer to him. "Ashley's cooking for us this summer."

"She is?" said Elf and regarded Ashley with doubtful eyes.

"Yes," said Tyler, "and she's a very good cook, too. Wait until you taste her cream puffs."

"I don't like cream puffs," said Elf in a small voice.

"Of course you do," said Tyler with a laugh. "Every little girl likes cream puffs."

"I want Shorty," said Elf.

Ashley had been watching the exchange between Elf and Tyler with growing anxiety. The introduction was not going well at all. Then, to her dismay, she saw Elf's lower lip begin to tremble and her eyes fill with tears. The child mutely looked down at the floor and some teardrops splashed onto her shoes.

"Sweetheart," said Tyler, bending down, "what is it?"

"I wore my dinosaur suit," said Elf, quietly sobbing, "just so Shorty could see it."

"We'll send him a picture," said Tyler.

"It's not the same," said Elf and buried her head against Tyler's leg.

Tyler straightened up and shot Ashley a look of frustration. His expression told her that he was as uncomfortable as she with this awkward turn of events. Clearly, he adored the little girl, but found it challenging to deal with such a sensitive child.

Just then, Josephine appeared at Elf's side.

"Oh, look," said Tyler, trying to distract his daughter, "here's your good friend Josephine."

The kindly older woman seemed to size up the situation at a glance. Gently, she took the little girl by the hand and spoke to her in a cheery voice.

"It's so good to see you, Elf," she said. "Come with Auntie Josephine. I've got a nice glass of orange juice for you over at my table."

With that, she led the child away.

As Ashley watched them cross the room, she saw Elf glance back over her shoulder. The little girl had such a look of disappointment on her tear-streaked face, Ashley's heart filled with empathy for her.

She felt, as well, an unexpected pang of rejection. She knew that it made no logical sense to feel that way. Still, she had to admit that she'd wanted Elf to like her. Oh, if only she could magically put Shorty in her place at that moment, she surely would have, just to please the little girl. Just then, her own eyes filled with tears.

"Oh, no," said Tyler with a groan, "not you, too." He

put his hands on his hips. ''One sobbing female per day
is my limit.''

Although his voice had assumed a tone of mock gruff-
ness, it contained a note of humor, as well.

Ashley was touched that Tyler was trying to jolly her
out of her distress, but it only made things worse. She
blinked, but it was no good. Tears began streaming down
her face.

''I'm sorry,'' she mumbled, wiping the back of her
hand across her cheek.

Hoping to mask her feelings, she tried to look busy. As
she picked up a pan, however, her arm accidentally
brushed against a container of hot oatmeal.

''Ow!'' she said, setting the pan back down with a thud.

''Did you burn yourself?'' asked Tyler.

''Yes, I think so.''

Suddenly, it was all too much for Ashley. The combination of last night's scene on the beach with Tyler, and
the disappointing first meeting with Elf, had overloaded
her emotions. The red welt that was now rising on her arm
had pushed her over the edge. The burn was just the excuse she needed, however, to flee Tyler's presence.

''I'd better go and take care of this,'' she said, referring
to her arm, and began walking away.

''There's a first-aid kit in the pantry,'' said Tyler. ''Let
me show you where it is.''

''Never mind,'' said Ashley, ''I can find it.''

Once inside the cool privacy of the pantry, which was
redolent with the spicy, reassuring fragrances of her trade,
Ashley closed the door and leaned against it. She squeezed
her eyelids shut and dug her fingernails into her palms,
trying not to cry again.

But it was no use. Streams of scalding tears were soon
flowing freely down her cheeks.

Presently, there came a knock at the door.

"Ashley," said Tyler's voice, muffled through the wood, "let me in." He rattled the doorknob.

Ashley kept her shoulder to the door and turned the lock.

"Please go away," she said, choking back her sobs.

"No," he said, "I will not go away. Now let me in. I want to talk to you."

"Well, I don't want to talk to you," said Ashley. "I—I need some time to myself."

"But I have to explain something," he said. "Besides, I want to check that burn."

Ashley moved away from the door and began searching for the first-aid kit. Finding it, she opened the box and rummaged around in it, looking for ointment and a bandage.

The doorknob rattled again.

"I mean it, Ashley," said Tyler. "Unlock this door or I'll break it down."

"How like a man," said Ashley, uttering the first thing that entered her head.

"What's that supposed to mean?" rumbled Tyler's voice through the crack.

"How like a man," said Ashley, "to threaten to use brute force when you can't have your own way."

Tyler muttered something unintelligible, then Ashley heard the sound of tumblers turning in the lock. Presently, the door opened to reveal Tyler standing there. He regarded Ashley from beneath lowered brows and held something up in his hand.

"Master key," he said.

He slipped the key back into his pocket, then he stepped into the room and closed the door behind him. He crossed the space between him and Ashley in a couple of strides.

"Now," he said, taking her arm, "what about that burn?"

"I can handle it," said Ashley, trying to pull away.

"Hold still," said Tyler, not unkindly, and grasped Ashley more firmly.

Submitting at last, Ashley watched in silence as Tyler gently applied some soothing ointment to the burn. Then he covered the spot with a bandage.

"There," he said, "you can take that off tomorrow. The burn's not too bad. It should heal in a day or two."

"Thank you," said Ashley.

Then, to her surprise, Tyler raised her arm to his lips and gently kissed the skin near the bandage.

"I'm sorry," he said, looking deeply into her eyes.

"It's not your fault that I burned myself," said Ashley.

"I don't just mean the burn," he said softly.

He pulled her close and wrapped his arms around her. With a small, involuntary cry, Ashley buried her face against his solid chest and accepted his comfort. He seemed to have a natural talent for making her feel better, a fact that only made the emotional tug-of-war within her all the harder to bear.

"Why all the tears?" asked Tyler, his breath warm against her temple. "It's not just because of your arm, is it?"

"Shouldn't you be checking on Elf?" said Ashley, drying her eyes.

"I will in a minute," said Tyler, smoothing his hand down her back. "She'll be fine with Josephine for now." He paused. "Why were you crying, Ashley?"

"I suppose it's several things," she said. "I feel so sorry for Elf, after what you told me about her last night. I've been looking forward to meeting her and making her feel welcome, but I think I must've really disappointed her just now.''

"What do you mean?" asked Tyler.

"I completely blew our introduction," said Ashley ruefully. "First, I misidentify her costume, and then I turn out to be the wrong person." She sighed. "Talk about a case of starting off on the wrong foot."

Tyler chuckled as he grazed her forehead with his lips and brushed some locks of hair away from her face.

"I think I should explain about Shorty and the dinosaur connection," he said, growing sober. "When Elf's parents died, Shorty took pity on Elf and went out of his way to cheer her up. He baked her special cookies, taught her how to play checkers, and lent her some of his books.

"One of the books was about dinosaurs," he continued. "For some reason, Elf fell in love with them, with dinosaurs." He laughed briefly. "Now it's practically all she can talk about. She even wants to be a dinosaur scientist, as she calls it, when she grows up."

"Yes," said Ashley, "she mentioned that."

"I think I can guess," said Tyler, "why she was so upset today when she learned that Shorty wasn't here. Shorty and his dinosaurs came to Elf's rescue when her world fell apart. Great big interesting animals—plus a very caring adult—can be a wonderful distraction for a little girl who's in a lot of pain." He hugged Ashley.

"So don't take her reaction personally," he added. "She'll get over it."

"I'll admit," said Ashley, stepping out of Tyler's arms and reaching for the first-aid kit, "that I felt kind of rejected." She looked at him. "Silly, isn't it?"

There was a long pause in the room. Tyler held Ashley's eyes with his and finally spoke.

"I'm sorry about last night," he said. "Everything I said seemed to upset you."

"You needn't apologize," said Ashley, replacing the first-aid kit on the shelf. "It isn't your fault that we have such different goals."

"Do we?" asked Tyler in a quiet voice.

"Of course, we do," said Ashley in a matter-of-fact tone. "You want to settle down and make a family, and I'm getting ready to pull up stakes and go live halfway around the world."

"Don't tie you down or fence you in, is that it?" said Tyler, studying her.

"You could say that," said Ashley, forcing a light tone into her voice.

"Now that you've got your freedom back, so to speak," said Tyler, referring to her broken engagement, "you want to see the world."

"I may as well," said Ashley with an unconcealed note of bitterness. Then she shrugged. "Anyway, I've always had wanderlust."

"It sounds to me," observed Tyler, "that what you're doing is running away, not giving in to wanderlust."

"Don't analyze me," said Ashley, more sharply than she intended.

"Sorry if I hit a raw nerve," said Tyler with a hint of impatience. "I seem to do that a lot with you." There was an uncomfortable pause. "I'm just trying to get to know you better, that's all. But, honestly, Ashley," he said, shifting his weight, "getting information out of you is like pulling teeth."

"I'd better get back to work," said Ashley, trying to brush past him. "Thanks for the first aid."

"You don't have to rush off," said Tyler, holding her back by placing his hand on her arm. "I told Mitch to take over for you at the steam table. Everything's under control out there.

"Tell me something," he added, drawing Ashley around to look at him.

"What?" said Ashley, her skin warm where his fingers grasped her.

"I'm curious about this China thing," he said. "You're going to be teaching in an orphanage—is that it?"

"That's right."

"The job sounds interesting," said Tyler. "Tell me more about it."

"It's a long story," said Ashley, hedging. "I don't think we have time right now."

"So give me the short version," he said, with a smile of friendly persuasion.

Ashley took a deep breath. Where to begin?

"Just before World War Two," she said, "my grandfather—that is, my dad's dad—took a job in Shanghai with an American oil company. Grandpa was still single back then. While he was there, he learned to speak fluent Mandarin.

"He became good friends," she went on, "with some local people who ran an orphanage. When he saw how poor the orphanage was, he decided to do what he could. He'd stop by with bags of oranges, and he'd help out with carpentry projects, for example."

"What happened when the war broke out?" asked Tyler, who seemed intrigued by the story.

"Like a lot of foreigners back then," said Ashley, "my grandfather was branded an enemy of the Communist revolutionaries, simply because he was a Westerner. They accused him of being a spy, but of course he wasn't anything of the sort. He was just in the wrong place at the wrong time, that's all."

''Was he arrested?''

''No,'' said Ashley, ''because when his Chinese friends heard that he was in danger, they hid him at their orphanage.''

''What a story,'' said Tyler, giving a low whistle. ''I assume he finally made it out of the country.''

''Yes, he did,'' said Ashley, ''again with help from his friends. One night, a produce truck smuggled him from the orphanage to the river. Once there, he got onto a fishing boat headed for Taiwan, where he caught a plane back to the States. His friends at the orphanage had set the whole thing up, at great risk to themselves, of course.''

''What an amazing tale,'' said Tyler. ''Did your grandfather ever consider writing a book?''

''I'm not sure if he did or not,'' said Ashley. ''What I do know is that he kept a diary while he was in hiding. Unfortunately, he accidentally left it behind when he was spirited out of the country.''

''Oh, no,'' said Tyler, ''what a shame.''

''For fifty years,'' said Ashley, ''our family naturally assumed that Grandpa's diary was lost forever.'' She laughed. ''Can you imagine our surprise when it showed up in the mail last winter?''

''You're kidding,'' said Tyler.

''No, I'm not,'' said Ashley, shaking her head. ''I happened to be visiting my Aunt Esther—she was Grandpa's daughter—when the package from China arrived at her house. We both nearly fainted when we opened it and found Grandpa's long-lost diary inside, along with a letter from a Mrs. Chun. She's the granddaughter of one of the men who helped my grandfather. She's also the current director of the orphanage.

''Anyway, Mrs. Chun,'' continued Ashley, ''explained in her letter that when the orphanage was recently refurbished, Grandpa's diary was found under a loose floorboard in his old room. It had been there all those years.''

''Amazing,'' said Tyler.

''It's just a shame,'' said Ashley, ''that Grandpa didn't live long enough to see his old diary again.''

''When did he die?''

''About ten years ago,'' said Ashley. ''By that time, of course, he'd long since met and married my grandmother and produced two children, my dad and my Aunt Esther.''

''Did he ever go back to Shanghai after the war?'' said Tyler. ''You know, to visit his old friends at the orphanage.''

''No,'' said Ashley, ''and that's the sad part. Grandpa never left the States again, even though the last thing he told his Chinese friends, before getting on that fishing boat, was that he'd return someday and repay them for their extraordinary act of courage.''

''What happened?''

''When Aunt Esther and my dad were still little kids,'' said Ashley, ''Grandpa had a stroke that left him partially paralyzed.'' She sighed. ''His traveling days were over, I'm afraid. He never got to go back to China.''

''That's too bad.''

''Eventually, what with one thing and another,'' said Ashley, ''Grandpa lost touch with his friends in Shanghai, but he often mentioned how much he regretted never having been able to go back to China to see them again. He owed them his life, he'd say, and it was true. If they hadn't hidden him during the war, he would've been thrown into prison, where he probably would've died.

''So you see,'' she went on, ''I actually owe those people my thanks, as well. If they hadn't helped get my grandfather out of China, he never would've married my grandmother, my father never would've been born, and I wouldn't have, either. I feel incredibly grateful to those kind, brave people at the orphanage. I'm alive today because of what they did for Grandpa.

"I was very touched," she added, "when Aunt Esther gave Grandpa's diary to me. She knew how much I loved it. I'd grown up hearing Grandpa's stories about his China days. Now that I've read his diary, I almost feel as if I've been through that ordeal myself."

"Of course," said Tyler, "you've been through your own ordeal lately."

"Yes," she said quietly, then cleared her throat. "You know, it's really ironic that the diary arrived when it did. In a funny kind of way, it saved my sanity."

"I'm not following you," said Tyler.

"Well," she said, moistening her lips, "the diary fell into my hands just about the time that . . ."

"Go on," he gently urged her.

"It arrived just about the time that Richard dropped his little bomb," she said.

"Richard?" said Tyler, raising one eyebrow. "Let me guess. Would that be your former fiancé?"

"It would," she said, taking a breath to steady herself. "After Richard broke off our engagement, I desperately needed something to distract me. I found myself reading Grandpa's diary to try to get my mind off my troubles. It worked.

"I wrote to Mrs. Chun," she continued, "to thank her for taking the trouble to track us down and return the diary. She's a wonderful person and we struck up a correspondence. When she mentioned in one of her letters that the orphanage needed someone to set up an English-language department in their new school, I jumped at the chance." She looked up into Tyler's eyes.

"It was exactly what I needed at the time," she went

on, swallowing an emotional lump that had formed in her throat. "A complete change of scenery."

"Away from everything that reminded you of—what was his name?—Richard," said Tyler.

"That's right," she said, blinking away some unshed tears. "Plus, it gave me an opportunity to do some good in this world, as well as carry out Grandpa's fondest wish. This fall, I'll go in his place to repay his Chinese friends for having saved his life all those years ago. It's the least I can do."

"He'd be proud of you," said Tyler, pressing her hand.

"I feel very committed to this plan, Tyler," she said in an earnest voice. "I've signed a contract, in which I've promised to devote the next two years to Mrs. Chun's orphanage. Unlike some people who break their promise," she said, alluding to her former fiancé, "I wouldn't dream of breaking mine.

"So you see," she continued, "you mustn't think that you can talk me out of this, because you can't. It also wouldn't be fair of me to start a relationship with you."

"I think we've already got a relationship," said Tyler softly, "whether you think it's fair or not."

"But I don't want to hurt you."

"Let me worry about that."

With that, he stepped closer, wrapped his arms around her, and gazed deeply into her eyes. He spoke with quiet fervor.

"Sweet Ashley," he said, cupping the side of her face in the palm of his hand, "give me just a word of hope. Let me believe that I have a chance with you."

"Tyler, please," said Ashley. "You know I can't do that."

"Do I have to follow you all the way to China," he said, smiling, "to plead my case?"

"You wouldn't," she said with a laugh, as she returned his tease.

"Don't be so sure," he murmured, then he lowered his lips to hers.

With her raw emotions so close to the surface, Ashley found it impossible to resist Tyler's embrace. For the next few moments, time and all of her troubles vanished into the air as she became aware of nothing except the sensations that were pulsing through her.

Tyler's nearness, his protective presence, distracted her from her thoughts. The flats of her hands registered the pleasantly rough texture of his shirt and the warm, firm muscles beneath the fabric. The only sounds in the room were of a clock softly ticking in the corner, the brush of Ashley's clothing against Tyler's, and two sets of ragged breathing.

At last, feeling flushed and weak-kneed, Ashley, with a little cry, stepped out of Tyler's arms.

"We—we have to stop this," she said, touching her enflamed cheek with the back of her hand. "Besides, I have to get back to work."

Tyler caught up her hand and kissed her fingertips.

"Just remember," he said with quiet determination, "if I have to follow you all the way to China—"

"Stop, Tyler," she said in consternation. "There's more to this than China."

"What do you mean?"

"I'm not what you think," she blurted. "I—I can't be what you want. I can't give you—"

She stopped, suddenly realizing that she couldn't bring herself to say any more on the subject. It was simply too distressing.

"Never mind," she went on hastily, her heart squeezing with pain at the look of puzzled dismay on Tyler's face.

As she turned to leave, Tyler's deep voice spoke behind her, filling the little room with a rumble of promise.

"We will continue this conversation," he said decisively, "another time."

Chapter Eight

A couple of mornings later, Ashley was working in the kitchen after breakfast when she heard a peal of childish laughter drift through the back screen door. Curious, she wiped her hands and went to have a look. There, behind the building, she found Elf in the company of Leo and Merlin. The child was picking wildflowers.

Ashley smiled with pleasure as she observed the scene unnoticed. The little girl crooned to Leo as she added flowers to the bouquet clenched in her small fist. Merlin was perched on her shoulder. Now and then, the raven tweaked one of the ribbons tied to the ends of Elf's braids.

''Merlin, don't,'' said Elf, giggling.

Ashley went outside and walked over to the trio. She hadn't had a chance to speak with Elf, beyond brief greetings at mealtimes, since the child's arrival. Now would be a good time to smooth out the rough edges of their initial meeting.

Elf looked up at her approach and Merlin hopped to the ground, where he'd just spotted a scrap of toast.

"Hello, Elf," said Ashley. She squatted down and ruffled the fur on Leo's neck.

"Hello," said Elf uncertainly, her demeanor suddenly shy and sober.

"Would you like some water for those flowers?" asked Ashley.

"I guess," said Elf, shrugging. Then she added, "I mean . . . yes, please."

"You're very polite," said Ashley, smiling.

"Daddy says I should be nice to you," said Elf, "because it's not your fault that Shorty's not here."

"I'm sure that Shorty wishes he could be," said Ashley. "Come on, let's get some water for those flowers."

In the kitchen, Ashley fetched an empty jam jar, filled it with water, and handed it to Elf. The little girl fussed over the bouquet, arranging the flowers with great care. Ashley's heart warmed as she watched the child's efforts.

"They're very pretty," said Ashley, admiring the flowers.

"They're for Daddy," said Elf, frowning in concentration. Putting the last flowers in place, she headed for the door. "I'd better go," she added. "Thank you for the jar."

"You're welcome," said Ashley. Just then, an idea popped into her head. "Elf, did you ever help Shorty in the kitchen?"

"Yes," said Elf, "I helped him all the time."

"How would you like to help me?"

"I . . . don't think so," said Elf, looking down at the floor.

"Oh, that's a shame," said Ashley. "I'm really busy this morning, and I don't have time to beat some egg whites." She gave an exaggerated sigh. "Well, I guess I'll just have to do it myself. You run along."

"Egg whites?" said Elf, looking up. A spark of interest ignited in her eyes. "I know how to beat egg whites." She hesitated, appearing to think the matter over. "Well," she added, "maybe I could stay a little while."

"Great," said Ashley. "I'll get you an apron."

An hour or so later, Tyler entered the kitchen. "Oh," he said, "there you are, Elf. I was wondering where you'd gotten yourself off to."

"Hi, Daddy," said Elf with a grin.

Swathed in an oversized apron, Elf was standing on a footstool at a counter, where she and Ashley were spooning batter into some muffin tins.

"You're not getting in the way, I hope," said Tyler, shooting a glance at Ashley.

"I'm not in the way, Daddy," said Elf, looking comically offended. "I'm helping Ashley."

Ashley and Tyler secretly exchanged looks of amusement.

"I beat some egg whites," said Elf, "and then I measured some applesauce. After that, Ashley needed me to help her sift some flour."

"I see," said Tyler, keeping a straight face.

"Now we're making apple muffins," said Elf, pointing to the tins. "They're for the afternoon coffee break." She looked at Tyler. "Daddy, I picked you some flowers. They're over there by the sink."

"Thank you, princess," said Tyler, looking at the little bouquet. "They're beautiful."

Picking up her full muffin tin, Elf stepped off the footstool and carried the tin across the room to Mitch, who was loading the big oven.

Tyler regarded Ashley. "Seriously," he said, "I hope she's not bothering you."

"Not at all," said Ashley. "She's a sweet little thing, and very intelligent." She looked over at the child. "I like her."

When she glanced back at Tyler, she caught the significant expression on his face.

"Now, don't get any ideas," she said, busying herself with another muffin tin.

"I'm afraid it's too late to warn me about that," drawled Tyler, speaking in a low voice that was meant for her ears alone. There was a warm glow in his eyes. "You know what I want." When Ashley didn't respond, he went on. "I think you've definitely broken the ice with Elf," he said conversationally. "In any case, it's nice of you to let her help out." Eyeing the muffin batter, he dipped his finger into the bowl.

"Hey," said Ashley, playfully swatting his hand. "No samples."

Tyler licked the sweet batter from his finger, and then shot her a smile that lit up his entire face.

"Sinfully delicious," he pronounced.

For a moment, time stood still for Ashley. In spite of the emotional wall that she had erected around her heart, a warm cloak of domesticity settled over her, momentarily creating the illusion that she and Tyler and Elf were a family. Although the illusion lasted for only an instant, it was powerful enough to leave an emotional lump in her throat.

Quickly she began spooning batter into the muffin tin, all the while chiding her imagination for putting such thoughts into her head. They served no purpose except to cruelly remind her of what she could never have.

"All done," said Elf. Proudly she showed Ashley the un-baked dinner rolls that she had brushed with melted butter.

"Oh," said Ashley, admiring the little girl's handiwork, "those are perfect. Now, into the oven they go."

It was several mornings later. By that time, Elf had gotten into a daily routine of dropping by the kitchen after breakfast in order to "help out." Ashley had cut an apron down to her size, and always had some simple tasks lined up for her to do.

"Now what?" said Elf, after watching Ashley slide the rolls into the oven.

"Now I have a very special assignment for you," said Ashley. She regarded the little girl with a mock serious look. "Can you decorate a cake?"

"A cake?" said Elf, her eyes growing big.

"Yes," said Ashley, "but it's not just any ordinary cake. This particular one is being prepared"—she leaned closer—"for a queen."

"There's a queen coming to the cannery?" said Elf, her mouth dropping open.

"That's right," said Ashley, "and we have to be ready for her. Now, you get up onto your stool and I'll get the cake."

A moment later, Ashley set a small cake down in front of Elf. Beside it she put a tray on which she'd placed a bowl of frosting, some food color, and several dishes of candy sprinkles, raisins, and chocolate chips.

"There," said Ashley. "Have fun."

"This cake . . ." said Elf, grinning up at her. "It's in the shape of a dinosaur!"

"That's right," said Ashley. "I made it just for you."

"*I'm* the queen?" said Elf, who seemed to be thoroughly enjoying their little game.

"Not yet, you aren't," said Ashley. "Before you can be a queen, you have to have a coronation."

With that, she pulled a crown out of one of the cupboards and held it over Elf's head. Earlier that day, Ashley had cut the crown out of cardboard, which she had then covered with foil. Now as she settled it into place, she intoned a solemn proclamation.

"I crown thee," she said, "Her Royal Highness Elf, Queen of the Dinosaurs." Then she gave the tip of Elf's nose a playful tweak. "There," she added. "Now it's official."

She laughed along with the delighted child, then watched for a moment as Elf got down to the serious business of decorating her dinosaur cake.

Thirty minutes later, Ashley was working at another counter when Elf called her over to have a look. The cake had been transformed. Elf had iced it with green frosting, then added rows of chocolate chips down each leg, colored sprinkles on the back and tail, and a plump raisin for an eye.

"It's a work of art," said Ashley, admiring the cake.

"I think we should eat the tail," said Elf, giving Ashley an impish look from beneath her foil crown.

"Great idea," said Ashley. "I'll get some plates, Your Royal Highness."

Later on, as they were eating, Elf regarded Ashley with a thoughtful expression on her face.

"Ashley," she said, "do you have any little girls at home?"

"No," said Ashley. "I don't have any children."

"I wish you could be my mother," pronounced Elf in a matter-of-fact voice.

Turning back to her plate, the little girl put another bite of cake into her mouth. She chewed and swallowed, then looked over at Ashley. Setting her fork down, she placed a small hand on Ashley's arm.

"Why are you crying, Ashley?" asked Elf. "Are you sad?"

"No, sweetheart," said Ashley, dabbing at her eyes with a paper napkin. "These are happy tears." She blew her nose and smiled over at the little girl. "That was a very nice thing for you to say."

A few minutes later, Tyler entered the kitchen.

"Daddy," piped up Elf, "come and see my dinosaur cake."

"That's very pretty," he said, walking over. Then, with a twinkle in his eye, he added, "But it seems to be missing a tail. What happened to it?"

"I don't know," said Elf, dissolving into giggles.

"Oh?" said Tyler, giving the child an owlish look. "Then how can you explain that frosting on your lips, hmm?" He tickled Elf. "I think that you and Ashley ate the tail."

"We did, Daddy," said Elf, adoring him with her eyes. "Ashley made the cake for me and I decorated it. She made my crown, too."

"I see," said Tyler, sending a grateful look Ashley's way.

"I'm the Queen of the Dinosaurs," said Elf, striking a regal pose. "Have some cake, Daddy."

"Just a bite, sweetheart," said Tyler, "and then I have to talk to Ashley for a minute."

Elf popped a morsel of cake into his mouth. Closing his eyes, Tyler chewed rapturously, as if the cake were the best thing he'd ever tasted. Swallowing, he opened his eyes.

"Mmm," he said, "that was scrumptious. Oh, look, here's Mitch. I'll bet he'd like some, too."

"Mitch," called Elf, "come and have a piece of my cake."

Tyler led Ashley out to the dining hall, where they could talk in private. They sat down across from each other at one of the tables. Ashley searched Tyler's face, looking for clues. What was this all about?

Ever since their conversation in the back pantry, the day she'd burned her arm, she'd been able to maintain a certain distance from Tyler. He continued to show up for the nightly card games, but he hadn't actively pursued Ashley with regard to their relationship. She was grateful for this respite, but knew that it was only a matter of time before he renewed his attentions.

"Something's come up," said Tyler.

"I can tell," said Ashley, noting the worry lines etched around his eyes. "What is it?"

"We'll be having an extra person at dinner sometime next week," said Tyler. "I just thought I'd warn you."

"It's not one of those developers, I hope," said Ashley with unconcealed dislike.

"No," said Tyler, shaking his head, "but it may as well be."

"What do you mean?"

"It's a fellow named Bjorn Harstad," said Tyler. "He's coming to talk business with me."

"Who is he?"

"Just the most powerful fisherman up here, that's who," said Tyler. "He came over from Norway about, oh, twenty years ago with just the clothes on his back. Now he owns one of the biggest fleets of fishing boats in Alaska. He's been selling his catch to Eagle Island for as long as I can remember.

"I've just learned, though," he continued, "that Harstad wants to pull his boats out of this area and start selling to our biggest competitor." He shook his head. "This is the last thing I would've expected."

"Why does he want to pull out?" asked Ashley, alarmed by the news.

"Harstad claims that Eagle Island isn't able to handle the volume anymore," explained Tyler. "I've invited him here to try to talk him into staying with us, but I'm probably wasting my time. Harstad's a tough businessman. If he thinks he can do better by moving his fleet, believe me, he'll do it."

"Didn't you mention to me once that you wanted to expand your cannery here?" said Ashley.

"Yes," said Tyler, "I've thought about that. An expansion would probably be enough to keep Harstad's business." He expelled his breath. "There's only one problem with that idea—I don't have the capital for such a project right now." He regarded Ashley. "If Harstad goes over to our competitor," he said, "it'll push us so far into the red, we'll never get out. We need his fish."

Ashley leaned forward. "You mean . . . ?"

"Eagle Island can't survive without Harstad's business," he said grimly. "If he pulls out, I'll be forced to sell this place."

"To those Seattle developers?" said Ashley, who could hardly believe her ears.

"To them or someone else," said Tyler in a weary voice.

"We've got to do something," said Ashley, with sudden passion. It was unthinkable that lovely Eagle Island—Tyler's paradise—should fall into different hands.

"Do you believe in miracles?" asked Tyler, with a wan smile. "Because that's exactly what it's going to take."

* * *

Over the next couple of days, Ashley could tell that Tyler had been deeply affected by the news of Bjorn Harstad's intention to start selling to Tyler's competitor. He had a preoccupied air about him, and Ashley guessed that his money worries were foremost in his mind. Her heart went out to him.

After breakfast one morning, Ashley realized that she'd left her wristwatch on the sill of an open window at her cabin. Removing her apron, she left the dining hall and walked up the path to fetch the watch. Not finding it on the windowsill, she went outside to search in the grass, believing that the watch had fallen to the ground. It was nowhere to be seen, however.

"Is this what you're looking for?" said a male voice from right behind her.

Ashley turned to find Tyler regarding her with an expression of amusement on his face. To her surprise, she saw that he was holding her watch.

"Thank you," said Ashley, accepting the watch from him and slipping it back onto her wrist. "But where did you find it?"

"Actually, Merlin found it," he said, "and then brought it to me."

"Oh, that naughty thief," said Ashley, laughing.

Once again, the raven's habit of pilfering shiny things had left her mind. The glitter of the wristwatch on the open windowsill must have been a powerful temptation. Ashley pictured the raven landing on the sill, plucking up the watch, and then flying it directly to his pal Tyler.

"I forgot about Merlin," she said, adding, "I'll have to be more careful."

Tyler started to leave and then paused. His face suddenly wore an expression of longing.

The cries of wheeling gulls reached Ashley's ears, and the warm air seemed to throb with expectation. As Tyler took a step closer to her, Ashley could tell that he was waging an inner struggle.

"Lately, I've been trying to give you a little space," he said, his deep voice husky with emotion. "I've kept my distance from you, but, at the moment, that's the last thing I want to do."

Closing the gap between them, he reached for her, molding his hands around Ashley's upper arms.

"Even in work clothes," he said admiringly, "you're an incredibly tempting woman. Every time I'm near you, I want to hold you and . . . and do this." So saying, he pulled her against him and sought her lips with his.

For several long, delicious moments, they clung to each other. Ashley reveled in the strong pressure of Tyler's enfolding arms, an embrace that made her feel warm and incredibly alive. The world and all of its troubles melted away like mist as Tyler's sensitive hands caressed her back and his mouth melded to hers. A shudder traveled through her as Tyler rained kisses onto her skin, from her lips to her cheeks and down the column of her throat.

Ashley's thoughts were jumbled. How easy it would be for the two of them to stay like this forever, there in the welcoming sunshine. A warning bell was sounding in her brain, however, and she firmly pushed Tyler away from her.

"Wait," she said.

In response, Tyler dipped near again and planted a searing kiss on the skin above her collarbone.

"Tyler," she insisted, pressing the flats of her hands against his chest. "Please stop."

He paused then and took a long, shuddering breath. Loosening his grasp, he gazed at Ashley's upturned fea-

tures and threaded his fingers through her hair, which was
billowing around her face in the sea breeze.

"What is it?" he said.

"We can't go on like this," she said. "It isn't fair to
you. I don't want to hurt you, Tyler. Please try to
understand."

There was a heavy silence. Then, with a soulful excla-
mation, Tyler dropped his hands to his sides and took
several long strides away from Ashley. When he whirled
around and regarded her, his face was a darkening mask
of anger. She had never seen him that way before.

"What is it with you?" he demanded hotly. "You return my kisses and then you act like you want me to get
lost. If you don't like me, just say so, but quit messing
with my mind."

"Tyler, please, I—"

"And don't give me that rubbish about not wanting to
hurt me," he grated from between tight lips. "The only
thing that's going to hurt me is seeing you walk out of
my life in the fall. Haven't you been paying attention,
Ashley? I'm crazy about you."

He stalked back to her and grasped her shoulders.

"Tell me you don't like me," he said, his low voice an
insistent hammer in her ears. "Go ahead. Look me in the
eye and say it." There was a pause. "Say it, Ashley, and
let's be done with it."

"You know I can't do that, Tyler," she cried. "You
know I like you, but—"

"But what?" he said, his voice harsh with emotion.
"It's that broken engagement of yours, isn't it? You're
afraid to get emotionally involved with me because that
other guy dumped you, is that it?" There was a painful
pause. "Is that it, Ashley? Because if it is, you're being
a fool."

"What are you talking about?" Her voice trembled and tears were stinging the corners of her eyes.

"You're letting one rotten experience affect your whole life," said Tyler, his voice agitated. "If that isn't being a fool, I don't know what is. Let go of all that, Ashley."

"I am letting go of it," she cried, "but in my own way. It was the worst experience of my life—can't you see that? I can't just bounce back, as if it had been nothing more serious than . . . than breaking a favorite teacup.

"I was engaged to be married, Tyler," she went on, her voice cracking with emotion. "I was in love. I didn't have a clue that Richard was going to break up with me."

"You must've seen it coming," said Tyler.

"No," she said, shaking her head, "I didn't. It was right out of the blue. One day, I was happily planning our wedding, and the next day, I was giving his ring back. How can you possibly know what that feels like?" She angrily blinked away her unshed tears. "So please spare me your lectures," she continued heatedly, "about being a fool and wrecking my life. It's not your concern and, frankly, I don't care what you think."

"Why did he break off the engagement?" demanded Tyler. "If I knew that, maybe I could understand what's going on with you."

"It's none of your business," she snapped, then inwardly flinched as her words hit their mark. A look of such hurt crossed Tyler's features that Ashley's stomach twisted painfully.

Just then, there came the sound of Mitch's voice calling out Ashley's name from the direction of the dining hall. Ashley automatically glanced at her watch.

"I have to get back to the kitchen," she muttered.

Then she gratefully made her escape, leaving Tyler

standing alone, an expression of mixed emotions on his face.

For the rest of the day, Ashley had trouble concentrating on her work. The memory of Tyler's kisses kept returning in images so vivid, she felt her lips tingle and grow warm as the sensations played back in her mind.

Just as disturbing, but in a different way, were Tyler's words of anger and accusation, which kept ringing in her ears. She couldn't blame him for being upset, she admitted to herself. Maybe she should make a clean breast of it and fill him in on the details—the unbearably distressing details—of her broken engagement. She'd tried to do so that day in the pantry, when she'd started to explain about not being able to give him what he wanted. Then she'd lost her nerve.

Pausing in her work, Ashley stared into space, wondering if she was up to the challenge of being completely frank with Tyler. She knew that candor was necessary for there to be a bond of trust and intimacy between a man and woman. She'd always longed for such a relationship, and suspected that, among the men she'd known, Tyler was unique in that respect. Instead of avoiding intimacy, Tyler was outspoken in his desire to get to know Ashley better.

''What am I doing?'' she muttered under her breath, and gave the onions she was slicing an impatient chop with her knife. ''You'd think I was falling in love with the guy.''

A couple of days later, Ashley had one of her rare afternoons off. Feeling the need to escape from the confines of the cannery for a while, she hiked along the beach, then struck out overland on her return.

About a quarter of a mile from the cannery, she made

an interesting discovery. On the bank of a small, grass-edged lake tucked behind a little hill, she found an old-fashioned Finnish sauna. Inside the rustic shack, there was a skylight in the sloped roof, two tiers of wooden benches, and a stove made from an oil drum. A neat stack of split wood and kindling completed the picture.

Oddly, the sauna had apparently never been used. The door of the stove stood ajar, cobwebs crisscrossing the opening, and there were no ashes in the grate.

Ashley straightened up from her inspection, brushed off her hands, and went back outside, carefully shutting the door behind her. She wondered why the sauna had never been used. She would like to relax in it herself, come to think of it. There were many evenings when her body ached all over from her long hours in the kitchen. Thirty minutes in a healing sauna would be just the ticket on days like that.

Taking a last look around, Ashley headed down the trail toward the cannery as a plan began forming in her mind.

It was twilight by the time she was standing in front of Tyler's office door. She paused before knocking. She and Tyler hadn't exchanged more than a few passing words since their emotional standoff behind Ashley's cabin, and she felt some hesitancy at being alone with him. At last, however, she mustered her courage and rapped on his door.

Chapter Nine

"Come in," rumbled Tyler's voice.

Ashley opened the door and entered Tyler's office, where she found him hard at work at his desk. He'd taken so few breaks lately, she thought to herself, and felt a stab of sympathy for him.

"Well, hello," he said, waving her toward a seat. "What brings you here?"

"I came to ask a favor," she said, sitting down. "I was just out walking and found the sauna up by the lake. I was wondering if I might use it now and then. Would you mind?"

"Not at all," he said with a shrug, "except that it can't be used. It's not finished."

"Oh, nuts," said Ashley with a little sigh. "I was really looking forward to it."

"My dad and I built that sauna when I was a kid," said Tyler. "The only thing it lacks is volcanic stones. You heat them up and then pour water over them to form steam. Dad and I had planned to go over to Tulikof Island to get the rocks, but we just never got around to it."

Ashley remembered Tyler pointing out the cone-shaped volcanic peak of Tulikof, steaming in the distance, on the evening that they'd hiked up the hill behind the cannery.

"Would you mind if I went to the island and brought some stones back?" she asked, mentally planning. "If that's all the sauna needs, I'd be happy to complete it myself."

"That's a great idea," said Tyler. "In fact, I'll run you over there myself after dinner tomorrow."

There was a long pause in the room.

"I—I'm not sure I want you to do that," said Ashley quietly, her hands clasped in her lap.

"What, are you afraid of me?" asked Tyler. Although he was frowning, the corners of his mouth twitched with amusement.

"Of course not," said Ashley, put off by his outspokenness.

She felt her face grow warm as a rush of mixed emotions flooded through her. Actually, she'd love to go out for a boat ride with Tyler, but she wondered if it was such a good idea.

"Well," said Tyler, studying her, "do you want me to take you to Tulikof or not? Hey," he added, with a twinkle of humor in his eye, "it might even be fun. Now, there's a concept."

They both laughed and the tension in the room vanished.

"You know," continued Tyler, a thoughtful expression on his face, "I've been wanting to take a little break. Your timing's good, Ashley. I haven't been to Tulikof in years, and I'd love to show it to you.''

His words were uttered with an air of such gracious invitation, Ashley hadn't the heart to turn him down.

"All right," she said, standing up, "I accept your offer. Thank you, Tyler."

"Let's take Elf with us."

"That's a good idea."

"Ashley," said Tyler, standing up and walking around his desk toward her, "before you go, there's something I want to say to you."

"What is it?" she said, turning to regard him.

"Sit here with me," he said, pulling up a second chair beside the one she'd just vacated. "Please," he added.

Ashley and Tyler sat down facing each other, their knees almost touching. Tyler leaned forward and took both of Ashley's hands in his.

"I want to apologize," he began, gazing into her eyes.

"For what?"

"For losing my temper the other day behind your cabin," said Tyler. "I let my frustration get the better of me and I'm sorry I spoke the way I did."

"It's all right," said Ashley. "I don't blame you for being angry."

"I've been doing a lot of thinking the last couple of days," he went on. "I believe it's time for some plain talk."

Pausing, he raised one of her hands to his lips and kissed her open palm. In a sweet, automatic reflex, Ashley's fingers closed over the spot, as if to protect a priceless token that had been placed in her safekeeping.

Tyler continued, his gaze holding hers. "I'm in love with you, Ashley," he said with a grave intensity that smoldered in his eyes and resonated in his voice. "I think

I knew I was going to fall in love with you the day you got here.''

"Tyler, I—"

"Shh, my darling," said Tyler, pressing a finger to her lips. "Please let me tell you what's in my heart." Once again, he took her hands in his. "I want to spend the rest of my life loving you and protecting you. It's all I can think about, but there's something I have to ask you."

"What?" asked Ashley, her heart pounding.

"Do you feel anything at all for me, Ashley?" he asked, his eyes searching her face. "Please tell me if I have a chance with you. I have to know—it's driving me crazy."

Ashley's eyes brimmed with tears, she was so moved by the soulful plea in his voice. She reached up and took his face in her hands.

"What a sweet man you are," she said, her voice trembling. "I do have feelings for you, Tyler." She paused. "There's something I have to tell you, though."

She lowered her hands to her lap, took a deep breath, and reached deep inside herself for courage. Looking into Tyler's eyes, she acknowledged what she'd long suspected, that she could bare her soul to him and he would listen with a sympathetic ear.

"Don't stop now," said Tyler, gently encouraging her.

"The other day," she began, moistening her lips, "you said that if you knew why Richard broke up with me, you might understand why I've been so reluctant to get involved with you." She looked at him. "I think you're right about that."

"Go on."

"I've been wanting to explain everything," she said, blinking away her unshed tears, "but it's so hard to talk about."

"I can see that," said Tyler softly, grazing her cheek with the backs of his fingers.

She hesitated, then plunged headlong into the telling.

"I can't have children, Tyler."

There was a long, heavy silence in the room. Ashley stared down at her hands in agony, caught between a feeling of relief at having finally told Tyler and one of dread at what his reaction would be.

At last, Tyler spoke. "He broke up with you because you can't have children?" he said, his voice giving no indication of his reaction to her news.

"That's right," said Ashley, her throat thickening with shame and embarrassment at the memory. "I'd come to terms with my situation years ago, and, frankly, it's never bothered me all that much. That is, not until Richard broke off our engagement.

"Right from the start," she went on, "I was very candid with him on the subject. I told him about it on our third date, in fact, so it wasn't as if he didn't know. He knew about it for over a year before he broke up with me." She looked at Tyler. "All along, I naively assumed that he'd even told his parents about it, but, as it turned out, he hadn't."

"You've lost me," said Tyler with a slight frown.

"Even though Richard claimed," said Ashley, "that my inability to have children didn't matter to him—we could adopt, he'd say—it turned out that it mattered very much to his parents.

"Richard comes from a very wealthy and powerful family back East, and his parents—his father, in particular—had some pretty definite ideas about passing on the family genes. Adopting children is simply not an option in their clan."

"That's so narrow-minded," said Tyler.

"Yes, it is," said Ashley, sighing. "But try telling that to a future father-in-law who can't abide the idea of compromising the family bloodline.

"So to make a long story short," she went on, "right before our wedding, Richard finally told his parents that I can't have children, and his father convinced him that I had a fatal flaw, as he put it. I think Richard tried to resist his father's objections, at first, but in the end he allowed himself to be persuaded. He was sorry, he told me, but his first loyalties lay with his family. When I look back," she added, "I guess I actually owe Richard's father my thanks."

"How so?"

"He helped Richard find the truth in himself," she said in a stony voice. "On the night I gave Richard's ring back to him, he admitted to me that he'd been deluding himself. He really did care, he said, about my not being able to bear his children. It did matter, and his father had helped him see that." She hesitated as the hurtful memories flickered in her mind. "To his credit, he had tears in his eyes when he told me." She paused. "It was then that I realized I was no longer in love with him. Shortly after we broke up, I heard that Richard had moved back East to be closer to his family. I assume he's already dating someone else.

"So you see," she concluded, regarding Tyler, "I have a fatal flaw. I can't have children. End of story."

"Stop talking nonsense," said Tyler with passion as he squeezed both of her hands. "The only fatal flaw I see is with this Richard guy. He can't have much of a backbone to buckle under to his father like that and let you slip through his fingers." He smiled, obviously trying to reassure her. "But his loss is my gain."

"Tyler," said Ashley in anguish, "aren't you listening to me? I can't give you a son or daughter. You've already told me that you don't want Elf to grow up as an only child, the way you did. You want her to have a little brother or sister, remember?''

''Sweetheart,'' said Tyler, lightly kissing her on the lips, ''we'll adopt.''

''That's what Richard always said,'' responded Ashley in a brittle voice. She pulled away from him. ''And I was naive enough to believe him.''

''It doesn't matter to me that you can't have children,'' persisted Tyler. ''Really it doesn't.'' He paused. ''You're apparently forgetting that Elf is adopted. That should prove something to you.''

''You'll change your mind,'' said Ashley, ''once you've thought about it. You're just feeling sorry for me— that's why you're saying these things. The last time I was with Richard, I saw the pity in his eyes. I swore that no one was ever going to look at me that way again.''

Tyler reached for her, sandwiching her face between his hands.

''Do you see pity in these eyes?'' he demanded, his voice harsh with emotion. ''Look at me, Ashley.''

''I am,'' she said, feeling emotionally bruised and painfully vulnerable.

''Do you see pity here?'' he repeated, his tone softening. ''Or do you see love?''

When she didn't respond, he drew her closer and kissed her, the caress of his lips engulfing her senses.

Finally, he pulled away from her lips at last and again gazed deeply into her eyes.

''I've been thinking about your job in China,'' he said, a practical tone entering his voice. ''I want you with me, Ashley, and not off on the other side of the world. I know the job at the orphanage means a lot to you, but couldn't you tell Mrs. Chun that you've changed your mind and won't be coming, after all?''

''I can't do that,'' said Ashley, shaking her head. ''You know I can't. I gave my word.''

''Well, couldn't you at least put her off for a few months?'' persisted Tyler. ''There must be some way that we can be with each other in the fall, instead of you flying clear to the other side of the—''

Just then, there came a knock at the door.

An expression of impatience at being interrupted crossed Tyler's handsome face. Arising, he strode to the door and opened it, revealing Bob, his foreman, standing at the threshold.

''Yes,'' said Tyler, all business, ''what's up, Bob?''

''Mr. St. Clair, Ashley,'' said Bob, greeting them both. Then he turned to Tyler. ''I was just wondering,'' he said, ''if you were finished with those inventory sheets we were talking about earlier.''

''Oh, yeah,'' said Tyler, rubbing the back of his neck. ''The inventory sheets. I've, uh, just about got that wrapped up. Give me five more minutes and I'll bring the papers down to you.''

''Okay,'' said Bob. ''I'll be in the warehouse.''

When Bob left, Tyler closed the door and spoke to Ashley.

''I'm afraid,'' he said, ''that we're going to have to table our discussion for now.''

''I have to go, anyway,'' said Ashley, standing up.

''Promise me that you'll think things over,'' said Tyler, taking her hand. ''I love you, Ashley. I want you with me and I couldn't care less that you can't have children.''

''I've heard all of this before,'' said Ashley with a sad little smile. '' 'I love you. I want you with me. It doesn't matter.' " She looked into his face. "I just don't believe it anymore, that's the trouble."

"No," said Tyler, a note of frustration entering his voice, "the trouble is that you've forgotten how to trust. I know I can change that if you'll just let me try." He gestured with his hand. "But if you run away to China, I'll never get the chance, will I?"

"I'm not running away."

"We both know you are."

An uncomfortable silence settled onto the room as the two of them stood, several feet apart, and mutely stared at each other. Tyler's final comment rang in Ashley's ears like a challenge.

Finally, mumbling something about setting dough for the next morning's breakfast rolls, she brushed past Tyler, opened the door, and made her escape.

Chapter Ten

Gusts of fresh sea air caressed Ashley's face the next evening as the skiff carrying her, Tyler, and Elf pulled away from the cannery. Once outside the bay, the boat gathered speed, the front end slapping smartly against the blue swells.

Ashley and Elf sat near the front of the skiff, with Tyler seated in the stern, his hand on the rudder. He was wearing wraparound sunglasses, of a style favored by pilots, and a weathered parka. The wind swept his hair back from his face, and the planes of his forehead reflected highlights from the slanting rays of the sun.

Trying to ignore how her heart skipped a beat at the sight of him, Ashley concentrated on the details of their errand. Their plan was to go to Tulikof Island, collect the necessary stones for the sauna, and then head straight back before dark.

Ashley drew her parka more closely around her and admired the raw beauty that was unfolding before her eyes. The heads of some curious seals broke the surface of the water a few yards to the right. Ashley pointed them out to Elf, who waved excitedly for her dad to look, too. Tyler gazed out at the seals, then grinned back at Elf.

The seals and wheeling seabirds, the fragrant salt breeze, and the sensation of starting out on an adventure suddenly filled Ashley with a surge of well-being. It felt glorious to share with Tyler and Elf the wonder of all that wild beauty. She could tell from the relaxed look on Tyler's face that he was enjoying the outing as much as she.

Elf was obviously savoring the experience, as well. Her mittened hands clung to the gunwale as she looked this way and that like an alert little bird, taking in everything around her with great interest. Whenever the boat bounced on the water, she squealed with excitement. Instinctively, Ashley hugged the child closer to her.

As they approached Tulikof, Tyler reduced their speed and angled around to the right, guiding the skiff toward a sheltered cove.

Ashley looked around. Green slopes soared skyward against a dramatic backdrop of blue Alaskan sky. Nesting murres and kittiwakes crowded the ledges of jagged, offshore sea stacks, the air above the stacks a swirling mass of bird activity. Dominating all was the conical shape of the volcano for which the island had been named.

The skiff glided into the cove. Waves purled softly onto a crescent of gray sand, frosting the shore with puffs of ivory foam. Tyler cut the engine and steered the skiff toward the beach. Then he tucked his sunglasses into his pocket and stepped into the shallow water. He was wearing rubber boots to keep his feet dry.

"Come on, princess," he said to Elf. "I'll carry you ashore."

After setting Elf down on the beach, where she immediately became absorbed in a search for shells, Tyler splashed back to the skiff.

"Okay," he said to Ashley, "you're next."

"Oh, I can make it on my own," she hastily replied. "It isn't far."

"Don't be silly," said Tyler, stepping nearer. "You'll get wet, and then you'll be miserable the whole time we're here."

Before Ashley could voice another word of protest, Tyler had scooped her up and lifted her into his capable arms. Her form rested against his body, the physical contact a powerful reminder of those other times he'd held her close. And kissed her lips, Ashley recalled with a faint heart.

Tyler stood motionless in the water, little waves making soft lapping noises against his boots.

"You needn't be so nervous," he said in a low voice. There was a wicked, teasing twinkle in his eye. "I'm not a pirate taking you off to my lair, you know."

"What makes you think I'm nervous?" said Ashley, feeling her cheeks grow crimson at his colorful imagery. At that moment, with his windblown hair and rakish smile, Tyler did remind her of an untamed adventurer of the high seas.

"I can feel you shaking all over," he observed. He gathered her closer. "Try to relax," he said. "Put your arms farther around my neck."

She hesitated.

"We're not moving an inch," said Tyler with a deep-throated chuckle, "until you hang on properly."

"Oh, all right," said Ashley, tossing her hair with a last little show of resistance. Then she complied by twining her arms more tightly around him.

"There, that's more like it," said Tyler, and splashed to shore.

"I like carrying you," he murmured at the beach.

"Yes, well," she said, wriggling, "you can put me down now."

With a show of reluctance, Tyler set her on her feet, but his arms remained around her. There was a potent silence as he looked down into her face.

"You're lovely," he murmured at last. "Your cheeks are all pink from the wind. And your hair, the way it catches the sun . . ." He chuckled. "Yes, I know," he said, silencing her lips with his finger, "you're about to tell me to behave myself."

He grew still then as he held her gaze, unspoken messages of love and yearning radiating from his eyes.

"I'm glad you found the sauna and asked to come over here," he continued presently. "It feels good to get away from the cannery and have a little fun."

Ashley couldn't remember when she'd ever seen Tyler so relaxed and mellow. Her heart went out to him as she realized with a wave of recognition just how much she'd come to like the man. Maybe she *was* falling in love with him. Surprised at her reaction, she drew away a little, needing time to think it over.

"Shouldn't we start gathering those rocks?" she said, gently bringing him back to their purpose for being there.

Tyler tied the skiff to a beached log, then he summoned his daughter, who was, by that time, busily digging in the sand. Elf ran over to them, breathless and bubbling with laughter. Grains of sand dusted her cheek and forehead. Tyler handed her one of the burlap bags he'd brought along.

"You can help us get the rocks, Elf," he said. "Come on, I'll show you where they are."

Tyler and Ashley walked along the beach in companionable silence as Elf ran ahead of them. Ashley looked back once and found herself comparing her and Tyler's two sets of footprints in the damp sand. Hers were the smaller and more shallow of the two, while Tyler's were deep and frankly masculine.

Weaving in and out of their tracks was Elf's little trail, a string of lively imprints that scampered now here, now there, like those of a joyful, bounding puppy.

Presently, they came to a former lava flow, where there were volcanic stones of just the right size for the sauna. As they made their selections, Ashley and Tyler talked of nothing in particular. Ashley had the feeling, however, that, even though their conversation centered on insignificant topics, there was an undercurrent of more meaningful communication pulsating beneath the surface.

"That ought to do it," said Tyler presently, and they hiked back to the boat, toting their bags.

"There's just one more thing to do before we leave," said Tyler, reaching into his pocket and taking out a camera. "We have to record this moment for posterity. You two go and sit on that log over there."

While Elf and Ashley positioned themselves on the log, Tyler placed the camera on a rock a few feet away and began setting the timing device.

"Are you two ready?" he said, looking over his shoulder at Ashley and his daughter.

"Ready," they both chorused.

"Okay," he said, running toward them, "here we go."

Tyler sat down on the log beside Elf, creating a pose that placed the little girl between him and Ashley.

''We've got about five seconds,'' he said, ''so everybody smile and say 'cheese.' ''

''Cheese!'' said everybody and laughed.

There was a faint whirring from the camera, then the sound of a click as the shutter opened and closed to snap the picture.

''That ought to be a good one,'' said Tyler, walking over to collect the camera and tuck it back into his pocket.

Ashley had to agree as she imagined the result. The photograph would show two laughing adults, a man and a woman, their heads touching as they nestled a merry-eyed little girl between them. The little girl clasped the woman's hand, and one of the man's arms was wrapped around both the child and the woman, in the classic and endearing attitude of the protective male.

Although millions of such pictures had probably been taken since the invention of the camera, Ashley felt that this particular one would always be unique and special to her. She felt a wave of affection for her two companions as she walked with Tyler to the waiting skiff. Elf ran ahead.

''I'll look forward to seeing that picture,'' remarked Ashley.

''I will, too,'' said Tyler, catching her eye. Then he added, ''After all, it's our first family portrait.''

All of a sudden, Ashley felt a warm glow in the center of her being, as if her relationship with Tyler had turned a significant corner. Perhaps she could believe, after all, in the possibility of somehow linking her life with his. She looked up into his face, feeling exposed and vulnerable, and he seemed to read everything that was there.

''Sweetheart,'' he said adoringly, and took her hand.

"What are we going to do?" she said, biting her bottom lip. "What's going to happen?"

She was referring to the coming fall, when she and Tyler would go their separate ways.

"I don't know," said Tyler, "but we'll figure something out."

Just then, there was the sound of distant thunder. A few fat raindrops fell to earth.

"Looks like we've got some foul weather blowing up," said Tyler, glancing skyward. "Let's get going."

The squall caught up with them ten minutes later on the open water. Dark, billowing clouds smudged the sky, blotting out the lowering sun and turning the sea to a murky leaden gray.

Ashley shivered as she squinted into the wind and rain. On their way to Tulikof, the sea spray had felt soft and refreshing against her skin. Now the salty droplets, driven by the wind, stung her face and caused her eyes to water. To her dismay, she quickly discovered that her parka wasn't as waterproof as she'd thought. Soon she was drenched by the rain.

Putting her own discomfort aside, she concentrated on protecting Elf from the elements. She found a small piece of canvas under the seat, which she wrapped around the little girl. Hugging Elf close, she sheltered her as best she could.

It was dark by the time their skiff pulled up to the cannery dock. The area was deserted. Tyler jumped out and tied up the boat, then he took Elf, snug and dry in her canvas cocoon, from Ashley's arms. Exhausted from their outing in the fresh air, the little girl had fallen sound asleep. Tyler rested her on his shoulder and reached out to help Ashley.

"Your hand's like ice," said Tyler, pulling her from the boat.

"I'm all right," fibbed Ashley through chattering teeth.

Just then, a tongue of lightning forked across the sky and bathed the scene in a burst of quicksilver. Thunder rumbled in the near distance and the rain began to fall even harder.

"You most certainly are not all right," said Tyler with a frown. He felt the sodden arms of her parka. "Why didn't you tell me you were getting wet? I would've given you my jacket."

"I'll b-be fine," said Ashley as a long, chilly tremor traveled the length of her body. "Here," she added, turning toward the skiff, "I'll g-get these rocks unloaded."

"Forget the rocks," said Tyler. "I'll take care of them later. Right now, I'm going to take Elf to Josephine's and you're going to hustle on up to my place and get into a hot bath. Chills like yours can lead to hypothermia. And if there's one thing I don't need, it's a cook on the sick list."

"Your place?" said Ashley, looking up at him in the dim light. "W-why your place?"

"Because I've got the only bathtub on the island, that's why," said Tyler. "What you need right now is a long soak in a tub to drive the cold from your body." He gave her a little push toward the office building. "Now get going. That's an order."

"What about you?" she said through lips that felt stiff with cold.

"I'm not soaked to the skin," he said. "Besides, I have lots of work to do. Go on, now. You'll have the place to yourself. The door's unlocked. Make yourself a fire, too."

As Ashley stumbled up the dock on numb feet, she debated with herself. Should she take Tyler up on his offer of hospitality? The idea of a long, hot soak in a bathtub certainly had wonderful appeal at the moment. Tyler had thoughtfully turned his apartment over to her, so privacy wasn't an issue.

She glanced in the direction of her darkened cabin, an uninviting shape huddled in the cold, driving rain, and recalled that her shower was often temperamental and ineffectual.

The thought of a cool-water shower decided the matter. Her mind made up, she turned toward Tyler's apartment over the store, already anticipating the luxurious feeling of sinking into a tubful of soothing hot water.

A few minutes later, Ashley closed Tyler's door behind her and clicked on a lamp. The illumination bathed the room in a warm amber light. She hung her wet parka on a peg. Then she rubbed her hands together and looked around. The place had an appealing, lived-in look about it. A couple of Tyler's shirts were tossed over the back of a couch, the floor-to-ceiling bookcases were crammed with volumes stacked every which way, and there was a coffee mug sitting on a table near a big stone fireplace.

Ashley ran her fingers along the arm of a soft leather chair that stood nearby. She could imagine Tyler sitting there, staring into the flames, his feet up and his handsome face awash in warm reflections. The room smelled like Tyler, she realized, a heady mixture of musky aftershave, coffee, fresh salty air, and an element that was pure male. Her hand drifted over his shirts on her way to the bathroom and she smiled to herself. She liked being in Tyler's cozy bachelor lair.

Later, feeling revived after her long soak in Tyler's bathtub, Ashley padded out to the fireplace and knelt down on the hearth. Her plan was to dry her hair in front of a cheery blaze before going to her cabin. She glanced at the clock on the mantel; it was still early. If Tyler kept to his usual routine, it would be several hours before he finally quit working and went upstairs to his apartment. There was little chance that he'd intrude on Ashley's privacy.

Ashley laughed under her breath as she piled paper and kindling together and reached for some matches. She wondered what Tyler would think if he walked in and found her wearing his terry cloth robe, which she'd found hanging on a hook in the bathroom. Her own clothes were soaked; donning the robe had been the only logical thing to do after her bath. She didn't think Tyler would mind her wearing his robe, but he might find it amusing to see how big it was on her frame.

Adding some logs to the fire, she watched the flames leap up and felt cozy and warm, right down to her fingers and bare toes. Then she turned off the lamp, pulled a couple of lap rugs from the couch, and made a little nest for herself in front of the fire. Her hair would be dry in no time.

Ashley awoke with a start sometime later. She sat up, her heart hammering in her chest. For a few moments, she felt completely disoriented. Where was she? Then she looked around and slowly expelled her breath as she recognized the dimly lit interior of Tyler's apartment.

Stirring up the coals, she tried to remember what had happened right after she'd made the fire. The combination of fresh air and exercise, and later the penetrating warmth of the bath, had made her feel relaxed and drowsy. She recalled laying her head down for a short rest, whereupon she must have drifted off to sleep. Now it was past midnight.

Scurrying into the bathroom, she was surprised to find that the lights didn't work. She pulled on her clothes and was preparing to leave, when she heard the sound of heavy boots stamping on the landing outside. Presently, the door was flung open.

A cold gust of wind, laced with rain, swept into the room, for it was still storming. Flames leapt up the chimney and cast flickering shadows onto the walls and ceiling.

Tyler entered the room and closed the door behind him. He was holding a flashlight.

"You're still here?" he said, obviously surprised at the sight of Ashley. He shrugged out of his parka and tossed it onto a chair. "I thought you'd be long gone by now."

"So did I," admitted Ashley with a touch of embarrassment, "but I fell asleep. Thanks for the use of your bathtub. I'm leaving now."

"I wouldn't, if I were you," said Tyler, kicking off his boots and shaking water from his hair. "The power's out. I've got my engineers working on the problem, but it won't be fixed for a while. There'll be no heat in your place, so you may as well stay here where it's warm, at least."

Tyler had a good point. Ashley certainly didn't relish the idea of plowing through the rain to her cold, dark cabin, where she'd have to stumble around and then crawl between clammy sheets.

Of course, it was a bit awkward being in Tyler's apartment that late at night, but she supposed that she could handle the situation if he could. Returning to her cozy pallet in front of the fire, she added more sticks to the flames.

"I'm glad you got this place warmed up before the power went off," said Tyler, gratefully rubbing his hands together. "That's cold work out there."

"You're soaked," said Ashley.

"Yeah," he said. "Think I'll put on something dry."

With that, he disappeared into the bedroom, emerging a few minutes later in a sweatshirt and jeans.

Every nerve in Ashley's body felt tensed and alert at Tyler's nearness. She concentrated furiously on the orange flames as he draped his shirt and pants on a chair to dry. Then she placed another log onto the grate and watched the flames lick higher. The rain pelted against the windows in a steady tattoo, and the wind scraped around the corners of the building. Outside, all was storm tossed, while inside there glowed a haven of warmth and safety.

Just then, Ashley stiffened as she heard Tyler draw up behind her.

Chapter Eleven

''Mind if I join you?'' rumbled Tyler's deep voice. ''Not at all,'' said Ashley.

She tried to sound matter-of-fact, as if it were an everyday occurrence for her to sit in front of a fire with a devastatingly handsome man who just happened to be her boss.

She moved over to make room for Tyler on the pallet and he sank down beside her.

''Ah, that feels good,'' he said, holding his palms toward the blaze.

Ashley covertly studied his profile. As he basked in the fire's primal warmth, he reminded her of a noble ancient lord, just returned from the hunt. The rugged planes of his face were bathed in a golden glow and his eyes reflected the dancing flames.

''So, here we are,'' he said softly, and with a trace of teasing humor at their unusual situation.

''Yes, we seem to be,'' said Ashley, with what she hoped was an air of nonchalance.

''What shall we talk about?''

''Oh, I don't know,'' she said, idly breaking a twig into little pieces and tossing them, one by one, into the flames. ''No, wait,'' she added, ''there is something. Tell me about your childhood. Did you spend every summer on Eagle Island?''

''Pretty much,'' he said. ''I had a great time up here as a kid. Then when I got a bit older, Dad gave me odd jobs around the place.''

''Such as?''

''I started out with small chores,'' said Tyler, ''like sweeping up the store or labeling boxes of salmon—that sort of thing. My dad figured that I'd learn the business better if I handled some of the responsibilities at a young age.''

''Your folks must've been very ambitious,'' observed Ashley.

''Yes, they were,'' said Tyler, ''especially my dad. Maybe too much so.''

''What do you mean?''

''Oh, never mind,'' said Tyler in a dismissive tone. ''Forget I said it.''

''No, please tell me,'' said Ashley. ''I'd like to hear about it.''

''Well, my mother always had time for me,'' said Tyler, ''but Dad never really did. He was totally absorbed in the process of making money, and that was about it, I'm afraid.

''Oh,'' he went on, ''he helped me with my homework now and then, and he showed me how to do things. I think he might've even loved me—in his own way. But I always got the feeling, especially when I reached my teens, that he thought of me more as a future business partner than a son.

"Take that sauna, for instance," he went on. "Dad and I started building it together. Then he got busy and that was the end of our project. I was thirteen at the time. Building that sauna with my dad was the best thing I'd ever done," he said with feeling. "Dad kept promising me that we'd take a skiff over to Tulikof and get the best rocks for it. Then we'd try out the sauna together, just he and I, but . . . it just never happened. I'm sure he didn't mean to disappoint me or let me down, but try explaining that to a kid."

"It still bothers you, doesn't it?" said Ashley, gently probing.

"Oh, not like it used to," he said in a lighter tone. "For years, I wouldn't even go near the sauna, then I kind of forgot it was up there. When you asked about it, it occurred to me that I'd held a grudge against my dad for long enough. It was time to forgive and forget and move on.

"It's funny how we carry stuff like that around inside without even realizing it," he added, tossing some sticks onto the fire. "Maybe if the sauna's finally completed and put to use, I can lay that old hurt to rest."

Neither of them spoke for several long, reflective minutes. The silence was punctuated by the musical pattering of the rain on the roof, the singing of the wind under the eaves, and the cozy crackling of the fire.

Ashley could hardly believe the avalanche of feelings that were cascading through her. In the short time that she'd been talking with Tyler that night, she'd learned a lot more about him, about the inner man and his most private thoughts and emotions. His personal disclosures brought him closer to her, a fact that caused her to feel a powerful wave of tenderness for him.

"Hey," he said, breaking into her thoughts with a little nudge of his elbow, "this isn't fair."

"What do you mean?"

"If I'm going to bare my soul," he said with a humorous air of mock tragedy, "so are you." He leaned toward her. "Come on," he coaxed. "Talk."

"Oh, you already know a lot about me," said Ashley.

It was true, for Tyler had learned, through loving persistence, more about her than she'd ever intended to share with anyone. She spoke again.

"I certainly identify with what you said about laying old hurts to rest," she said. "I'm still working on that one."

"Let me help," he said softly, and kissed the fire-warmed palm of her hand.

Without warning, some tears fell from Ashley's eyes and ran down her cheeks. Tyler wordlessly wrapped his arms around her and pulled her against him.

It felt wonderfully comforting to be held next to Tyler in the firelit room. Even through the pain of remembering the circumstances surrounding her broken engagement, and the disillusionment that followed, Ashley noted with a poignant stab of gratitude that Tyler seemed to have an instinct for knowing how to respond to her.

At that moment, in a flash of crystal clarity, Ashley knew that she was deeply in love with Tyler. The knowledge filled her with awe, and she mentally paused to examine it, as if she'd unexpectedly stumbled onto a rare and lovely gem in her path. Her crying ceased.

Unwrapping his arms from around Ashley for a moment, Tyler added more wood to the fire. Then he resumed his posture of holding on to her.

"You know something?" said Ashley, drying her eyes and gratefully snuggling against Tyler once more.

"What?" he said, tracing his thumb along her jawline, then smoothing her hair back from her brow.

"Talking with you like this," she said in a voice that spoke of the twinkle in her eye, "is much more pleasant than fighting with you."

"I couldn't agree with you more," he said, with an earthy chuckle.

Then, gently he pulled her to him. She was soft and yielding. He studied her face with the lingering gaze of a man who has found the most pleasing sight in the world.

"But we aren't going to talk all night, I hope," he added and lowered his mouth to hers.

"You're trembling," he said presently, breaking the delicious bonding of their lips.

His warm breath fanned Ashley's face. One of his arms cradled her head, while his other arm curved possessively around her waist. He reached out and stroked her cheek.

"Dear Ashley," he whispered. Then he rained kisses onto her lips, cheeks, and neck.

Ashley reached up and laced her fingers through the luxuriance of Tyler's dusky hair. Every nerve, every sense seemed fine tuned, sharper and more receptive than they'd ever been to every little sound, scent, and touch. She'd never before felt so drawn to a man as she was just then to Tyler. At that moment, he was the very center of her universe.

She opened her eyes and drank in his features. Then, following her instincts, she kissed Tyler's neck, where his pulse beat rapidly.

"You know, I was just thinking," said Tyler presently,

"about how I believed at first that you wouldn't be able to handle the work up here. You've certainly proven me wrong about that."

He swooped his head low to kiss her once more. His lips moved restlessly over hers, a gentle caress that stirred her senses.

"I didn't know until I met you," he murmured, "how distracted I could be by a woman, how . . . greedy she could make me feel." Tyler gathered her to him for yet another kiss.

At that moment, Ashley experienced a sweet yearning such as she'd never felt before. As she had on Tulikof Island, she believed that she and Tyler could somehow forge a life together. Acknowledging her love for him in her own heart made all the difference in the world, she realized with a warm glow. Love was the element that gave her hope.

Just then, another noise besides the rain and the crackling of the fire came to Ashley's ears. Brought sharply back to reality, she opened her eyes, suddenly tense and on guard.

No doubt about it, there were footfalls sounding on the stairs leading up to Tyler's door. Tyler apparently heard them, too, for he raised his head and appeared to be listening.

Just then there was heavy pounding at the door.

"Mr. St. Clair," someone called out.

Ashley recognized the voice of Erik, one of Tyler's engineers.

"It must be something about the power," muttered Tyler.

He and Ashley moved apart. Ashley scrambled to her feet, her heart hammering. She couldn't imagine a more embarrassing situation than being seen in Tyler's apartment at that time of night. She dove toward the bathroom, where, to her relief, she found that the power had been restored.

Hearing Erik leave at last, Ashley cautiously emerged from the bathroom.

"You're not leaving, are you?" said Tyler softly, and reached out his hand to her.

"Yes," she said, "I think I'd better." She walked to the door and pulled on her soggy parka. "I'm actually relieved that Erik dropped by when he did," she continued, gathering her coat around her as she prepared to plunge out into the dark.

"Why do you say that?"

"Well," said Ashley, making a helpless little gesture with her hand, "we were getting a little carried away just then, don't you think?" She brushed some hair away from her face.

"Maybe that's just what we both need," said Tyler.

They stood in silence for several moments, staring into each other's eyes. Then Tyler stepped toward her. He slipped his arms around Ashley's shoulders and pulled her near.

"You're worth waiting for," he said with feeling. "And if that's how you want it, that's the way it'll be. You know how much I care for you."

"Oh, Tyler," said Ashley, "I care for you, too, but we're going our separate ways in the fall. What's the point of starting something we can't finish?"

"What do you mean?"

"How can we continue a relationship," said Ashley, "with me on one continent and you on another? All of the letters and phone calls in the world can't make up for not being together."

"I certainly agree," said Tyler.

"And even if you truly didn't mind about my not being able to have children, I—"

"I told you it doesn't matter to me," said Tyler with passion. "Why won't you believe me?"

"All right," said Ashley, biting her bottom lip, "I believe you. But even so," she continued, "what's going to happen to us at the end of the salmon season?" She looked at him. "Do you see a way out of this dilemma? Because I don't."

A chilly draft suddenly wafted under the door, sending shivers down Ashley's spine. Tyler dropped his hands from her shoulders and fixed her with an unblinking gaze.

"You're just going to have to tell Mrs. Chun," he said, "that you're not coming, after all."

"I signed a contract, Tyler."

"Contracts can be broken."

"I can't believe you're saying this," she said, sadly shaking her head. "Even if I didn't have a contract to work at the orphanage, I wouldn't break my promise to them. You, of all people, should understand that."

"What do you mean?"

"Think back, Tyler," she said. "Do you recall the night we walked up the hill behind the cannery?"

"Yes."

"You made such a point," she said, emphasizing her words, "of getting me to commit for the entire season, remember? You wanted me to give my word and keep it."

"All right," he said, raking an impatient hand through his hair, "I remember, but this is different."

"No, it's not," she said. "Mrs. Chun and the others are counting on me. I can't just suddenly change my mind."

"It looks like I'm going to have to follow you there, then," he said, giving her a half-smile.

"Don't, Tyler," she said in a small voice. "You've said that before, but I'm not in the mood to joke about this."

"Who's joking?"

"What, you're going to just walk away from your canneries, one of which is in serious financial difficulties?" she said. "And what about Elf? Where does she fit into such a crazy scheme? Are you going to drag her off to China with you?" She slowly shook her head. "No, Tyler, it won't work. You can't abandon your commitments, and neither can I."

"There must be a way," he said.

A painful silence hung in the air. Ashley could've wept when she compared the present mood of discouragement with the soaring joy that she and Tyler had felt in each other's arms a few moments before. Surely, there was something she could say to make the situation better, but her mind was drawing a blank.

It didn't help, either, to see the bleak expression on Tyler's features. His final words rang in Ashley's ears like a litany of false hope, for she could read in his face that he didn't see a solution to their problem any more than she did.

She parted her lips to speak, for she hated to leave on such a sour note. Before she could frame a comment, however, Tyler broke the silence.

"Go on," he said, fatigue showing in his eyes. "Go on to your cabin and get some sleep. We'll talk about this another time."

Miserable, Ashley opened the door and left.

Chapter Twelve

By morning the storm had moved on, leaving behind rain-scented air, blue skies, and a calm sea. After breakfast, Ashley found the volcanic stones from Tulikof Island piled behind the dining hall. As she was looking at the stones, she recalled the pleasant, magical trip with Tyler and Elf.

Then she remembered her and Tyler's heated discussion in his apartment, and her feelings of discouragement over their situation returned in full force. If she could only think of a compromise that would resolve their dilemma. She prided herself in not having a defeatist attitude, but, short of commuting by plane between Shanghai and Seattle—not an option to be taken seriously—Ashley could see no resolution to their problem.

Just then, Tyler's voice interrupted her thoughts.

165

"I see you found the rocks," he said in a conversational tone.

Ashley turned to regard him. He looked tired. Had he slept at all? She noted the beard stubble on his cheeks. He hadn't even taken time to shave that morning, she realized, and felt a wave of tender concern for him.

"Yes," she said, "thanks for hauling them up here."

She paused, uncertain how to proceed, but wanting to somehow smooth over last night's rough spots. Then an idea came to her.

"I hope you'll help me finish the sauna," she said.

"I don't know," said Tyler. "I'm pretty busy."

"But it was your project to begin with," said Ashley, determined not to be put off. "You should be there when the sauna's fired up for the first time. Besides, I thought you wanted to do it. You talked last night about laying old hurts to rest, remember?"

"Yeah, I remember," he said. "Let me take a rain check, okay? Right now," he went on, "I need to grab a shower and shave." He rubbed his palm across his cheek. "There's a plane coming this morning to take me to Bristol Bay. I have to check on our canneries up there."

"Will you be gone long?" asked Ashley, disliking the idea of his being away.

"Three or four days at the most," he said. "Bob and Josephine will be in charge here until I get back."

"I'm not going to fire up the sauna without you," said Ashley decisively. "It's only right that you be there the first time. I'll wait until you get back."

The next few days dragged by for Ashley. The island felt so empty with Tyler away. Even Leo and Merlin seemed to react to his absence. They hung around the kitchen door more than usual, as if at loose ends.

Everywhere Ashley looked, she was reminded of Tyler.

It was strange to glance toward the dock, for example, and not find him standing there, chatting with the fishermen or members of his crew.

His customary place in the dining hall seemed especially vacant. More than once, Ashley caught herself looking in that direction, expecting to see Tyler. When her eyes fell, instead, on an empty seat, a twinge of disappointment would ripple through her.

Ashley didn't have to search long to discover why she missed Tyler so intensely. She was in love with him—it was as simple as that. She knew now that the seeds of that love had been planted during her first week on the island. Although she'd resisted falling in love with Tyler, the idea had grown in her over time, nourished by the many no-holds-barred conversations the two of them had shared. Those conversations had created a bond of intimacy between them. It would be virtually impossible, Ashley reflected, not to fall in love with a man who could display such trust and such a willingness to bare his soul.

As the days crept along, Ashley's feelings for Tyler deepened. At the same time, her concerns about their future increased. Since it was patently obvious that Tyler could not accompany her to China, perhaps she should give some thought to somehow, some way, diplomatically extricating herself from her agreement with the orphanage. As she'd told Tyler, it was against her principles to break her word, but there might be something that she'd overlooked.

As she was mulling these matters over, a letter arrived from Mrs. Chun. On delicate blue paper, Mrs. Chun expressed her warmest gratitude to Ashley for agreeing to come to Shanghai to help the orphanage start its school. The staff members, read the letter, were planning a banquet to celebrate Ashley's arrival, and the children were preparing some musical entertainment especially for her. The staff and the children could hardly wait to meet such a kind and generous woman in person.

''Dear friend,'' added Mrs. Chun toward the end of the letter, ''your presence will truly honor us.''

Tucked in with the letter were several snapshots of some of the orphans.

As Ashley studied the open, friendly faces of the girls and boys—innocent little folk without mothers or fathers—her heart constricted with guilt. How could she even consider not following through on her agreement? It was unthinkable. She would go to work at the orphanage in the fall and that was that.

''Have you got a minute, Ashley?'' said Josephine, poking her head into the kitchen during dinner the next night. ''Mr. Harstad wants to meet the chef.''

Ashley was putting the finishing touches on the dessert, a huge cake smothered with whipped cream. Crowning the confection was a layer of fresh salmonberries, which she and Elf had picked that afternoon on the hillside behind the cannery.

It had been a hectic day. Right after breakfast, Ashley had heard the roar of an arriving seaplane. Rushing to a window, she'd seen Tyler descend from the craft. Her heart beat faster at the sight of him. It was wonderful to have him back at the cannery.

Then a second man stepped from the plane, a stranger whom she guessed was Bjorn Harstad. Recalling that Harstad was the powerful fisherman who was threatening to sell his fish to Tyler's competitors, Ashley watched anxiously as the two men headed in the direction of Tyler's office.

Later that morning, she learned from Josephine that

Tyler had headed home via Kodiak, where he'd run into Harstad. Because they were scheduled to meet anyway, the two men decided to share a plane back to Eagle Island. Since their arrival, they'd remained sequestered in Tyler's office. When they still hadn't emerged at lunchtime, Ashley sent Mitch over with a tray of sandwiches and coffee.

When evening arrived, the two men finally reappeared. Ashley saw them strolling toward the dining hall, still deep in conversation. With a preoccupied air, Tyler sketched a wave in Ashley's direction as he passed by the open kitchen door. Remembering how much Harstad's continuing business meant to the future of Eagle Island, Ashley responded by holding up her crossed fingers and giving Tyler a hopeful smile. She was dying to know how the discussions were going, and was frustrated at not being able to read a single clue on Tyler's face.

Ashley looked up from the cake.

"Sure, I can spare the time," she said, answering Josephine, "now that this is done." Giving the cake a last critical look, she called over to her helper. "Please take this out to Mr. St. Clair's table, Mitch."

"What in the world is that sinful-looking concoction?" asked Josephine, watching Mitch bear the dessert away.

"It's a Norwegian soggy cake," said Ashley, wiping some cream from her fingers.

"Soggy?" said Josephine with an inquiring glance.

"The bottom layer's liberally sprinkled with sherry," explained Ashley. "It's a very popular dessert in Norway. I thought Mr. Harstad might enjoy having some, since he's from over there."

Josephine's eyes glowed with admiration as she studied her young friend.

"Ashley," she said, "you're absolutely brilliant."

Ashley gave a self-conscious laugh. "What do you mean?" she said, removing her apron.

"Cooking a Norwegian dinner tonight for Mr. Harstad," said Josephine, "was such a good idea. Why, he's been raving about the food all evening. That's why he wants to meet you." She grinned. "He says he hasn't tasted some of those dishes since he left his little fishing village. The man's getting downright nostalgic out there." She paused. "How'd you know what to serve, anyway?"

"I catered a Sons of Norway banquet last summer," said Ashley, "and I happen to have the recipes with me. Norwegians eat lots of fish, and goodness knows we have plenty of that," she added with a laugh. "So it wasn't all that difficult to work out tonight's menu.

"Pulling it off at the last minute was the only tricky part," she went on, glancing in the direction of the dining hall. "I hope Mr. Harstad likes the cake."

"Oh, I'm sure he will," said Josephine with a decisive roll of her eyes.

"I just had to do something," said Ashley with passion. "I couldn't let him deliver a death blow to this cannery without putting up a fight."

She gestured with her hands as she recalled her initial feelings of helplessness.

"But I asked myself," she went on, "what can *I* possibly do to persuade Harstad to continue doing business with Eagle Island? After all, I'm only the cook here." She smiled. "Then I remembered an old saying."

"What old saying?"

"The one about the way to a man's heart being through his stomach," said Ashley. "It occurred to me that some old-fashioned Norwegian hospitality might put Mr. Harstad into a positive frame of mind. That way, perhaps he'd be more receptive in his discussions with Tyler." She gave a little shrug. "I admit it's a long shot, but it doesn't hurt to try."

"I think your plan's working," said Josephine, nodding sagely at Ashley's logic. "Harstad has a gruff exterior, but he's very sentimental about his Norwegian roots. You've put him into a receptive mood, all right. Come on, I'll show you what I mean."

Harstad and Tyler stood up as the two women approached their table. Ashley felt her color rise as her gaze met Tyler's. He looked particularly handsome that night, in a cobalt-blue shirt that accentuated the intense color of his eyes.

"So this is the little lady who knows how to cook Norwegian-style," boomed out Harstad, blotting some whipped cream from his lips.

Bjorn Harstad was a thickset man of medium height. He had a rough thatch of blond hair going to gray, a ruddy fisherman's complexion, and a gold front tooth that gleamed whenever he smiled. His speech was richly accented with the melodic Norwegian tones of his younger days.

As Tyler deftly handled the introductions, Ashley noticed out of the corner of her eye that a big chunk of her soggy cake had already vanished, and that the two men had helped themselves to seconds. Seating herself with Harstad and Tyler, she joined them in some light conversation while Josephine ushered Elf off to bed.

A few minutes later, Mitch came to the table with a carafe of fresh coffee. His arrival reminded Ashley that she still had some things to attend to in the kitchen, so she politely excused herself and stood up to leave.

As she was walking away from the table, she overheard Harstad say something to Tyler. She didn't catch all of the remark, except for the words "financial backing" and

"expansion." At that moment, something—she wasn't
sure what—made her turn her head and look back. As she
did so, she saw Tyler motioning for Harstad to be quiet.

When her eyes met Tyler's, an unexpected chill ran
down her spine. The guarded look on his face sent a feeling of uneasiness spreading through her. It was clear that,
for some reason, he didn't want her to hear what he and
Harstad were talking about and felt sheepish at having
been caught in the act of suppressing Harstad's comment.
Ashley returned to the kitchen, wondering what was going
on.

By the time she'd finally turned off the kitchen lights
and was heading for her cabin, Ashley had put two and
two together. Tyler's hush-hush behavior with Harstad
could only mean one thing: He had persuaded the fisherman to provide financial backing for an expansion at Eagle
Island, and he was still working out how to break the news
to Ashley.

She had to admit that it was a brilliant move on Tyler's
part. Harstad, a shrewd investor, from the sound of it,
would help create a bigger facility for his catch and would
thus continue selling his fish to Tyler. Tyler, on the other
hand, would get the expansion he'd been wanting, as well
as save his island. Yes, reflected Ashley, it was a very
smart deal.

The problem with such a plan, of course, was that an
expansion project would keep Tyler even more tied down
than he was now. Although Ashley had resigned herself
to the fact that she and Tyler would go their separate ways
after the fishing season, she had to admit that she'd been
secretly hoping for a miracle to change that.

In light of today's developments, however, the possibility of their forging a future together seemed out of the
question. In the fall, when Ashley flew to Shanghai, Tyler

would be completely caught up in the details of remodeling, working hard to ensure that the cannery would be fully functional again by next summer's fishing season.

As Ashley slowly walked up the path toward her cabin, she could picture Tyler with blueprints spread out on his desk, carpenters and engineers coming and going, and boats arriving with materials for the new additions. An exciting and busy time lay ahead of Tyler, and, in her heart, Ashley wished him well.

As she unlocked her door and went inside, however, a great heaviness settled over her, for she knew what the cannery expansion would do to her and Tyler's relationship. By the time he'd finished the project, the better part of a year would have slipped away and his memories of Ashley would have surely dimmed. What was the old saying? Out of sight, out of mind.

In the meantime, he'd no doubt meet and date other women while commuting between Seattle and Eagle Island. Ashley recalled how candid he'd been about his eagerness to marry. Hadn't he already made it clear how much he wanted a wife, as well as a mother for Elf? Why would he want to put off his heart's fondest desire for two long years while Ashley fulfilled her obligation overseas? Such a scenario was obviously out of the question and who could blame him.

Suddenly, as she was mechanically getting ready for bed, Ashley felt bitter tears streaming from her eyes. She imagined that, in spite of Tyler's professed love for her, it would be easy, in the end, for him to lose interest, bow to practicality, and turn his attentions elsewhere. Eventually, he would forget all about her, but she would never forget him or his dear little daughter. Picturing Tyler and Elf in her mind, Ashley felt her heart constrict with pain.

How she would miss them both. Oh, how she would miss them.

Later that night, Ashley looked up in surprise from where she was sitting on the edge of her bed listlessly toweling her hair dry. She'd just stepped from the shower and was wearing a long velveteen robe that was belted around her waist.

Wondering who could be knocking at that hour, she padded across the room in her bare feet and opened the door.

"Tyler," she exclaimed.

His tall body, framed by the night's ebony darkness, filled the doorway. He was standing with his weight on one foot, his arms loosely crossed over his chest and his shoulder resting against the doorjamb.

For a moment—in his open-collared shirt and faded jeans, which fit his long legs like a denim glove—he reminded Ashley of an arrogant cowboy. She felt a familiar tightening in her throat and a singing in her blood at the sight of him.

There was an awkward silence as she stared up into his face for a heartbeat or two. Finally, Tyler slanted a smile in her direction and spoke.

"Look, I know it's late . . ." he began.

In frank male assessment, his eyes swept over her damp hair and informal attire.

Ashley's hand automatically went to her throat, for she suddenly felt unprepared and exposed, her face washed clean of makeup, her form clad only in a robe.

"Harstad and I just finished our business," continued Tyler. "I'd like to tell you about it." He glanced into the cozy, lamplit room behind her. "Mind if I come in?"

Ashley moistened her lips. "No, I guess not," she said, keeping her voice steady.

She stepped aside and allowed Tyler to brush past her into the cabin. She hesitated a moment, her hand on the knob. Then, reining in her reluctance about hearing Tyler's news, she closed the door and joined him on the wicker love seat, where he'd settled back with his legs comfortably stretched out in front of him.

"I appreciate what you did tonight," he said, turning his blue-eyed gaze on her. "Serving a Norwegian dinner was a brilliant idea."

"Oh, I didn't do that much," she said with a shake of her head, yet she felt a small glow of pride at his praise.

"No, really," said Tyler. "Harstad and I have just hammered out the final details of an agreement, and I insist that you take some of the credit." He gave a short burst of laughter. "Who could resist a business proposal after two helpings of soggy cake?"

"I'm very happy that you and Harstad worked things out," said Ashley, forcing a smile onto her face. "That's wonderful news."

"I've been dying to tell you all about it," said Tyler, reaching for her hand. "I wanted to share the news with you in my own way, but Harstad almost let the cat out of the bag tonight."

"Yes," said Ashley, drawing her hand away, "I overheard part of your conversation." She took a shaky breath. "You must be so excited to know that you're going to be able to expand your cannery here."

"Expand the Eagle Island cannery?" said Tyler. A puzzled expression crossed his features. "What are you talking about?"

"It's all right, Tyler," she said. "I already know what's going on."

''Well,'' he said with a bemused chuckle, ''would you mind filling me in?''

''I heard Harstad say something about financial backing and expansion,'' said Ashley. ''He's obviously putting up the money to help you enlarge your facility here.'' She looked at him and added in a sincere voice, ''Congratulations, Tyler. You won't have to sell Eagle Island, after all.''

''Well, you've got that part right, at least,'' said Tyler, smiling. ''I won't have to sell the island. I'm incredibly thankful for that.

''And, yes,'' he went on, ''Harstad has agreed to put up some financial backing, but not to expand the cannery. When he mentioned expansion, he was talking about something completely different.''

''What?'' she said, suddenly confused. ''I don't understand.''

''I'd better explain,'' said Tyler. ''Yesterday morning, when I left Bristol Bay, I flew to Kodiak to see Ray Johnson, an old college friend of mine. Ray's a fish broker. He buys and sells fish all over North America. A couple of months ago, he'd run an idea past me, but I wasn't interested at the time. Now I am, and I wanted to discuss it with him.'' He paused. ''Are you with me, so far?''

''I think so,'' said Ashley, but she was not at all sure where their conversation was leading.

''Last night, while Ray and I were having dinner,'' continued Tyler, ''Harstad came into the restaurant. I invited him to join us and the three of us got to talking about this idea of Ray's that I mentioned.

''It turns out,'' he went on, ''that Ray wants to get involved in the expanding overseas market. That's what Harstad was referring to tonight, the expansion of foreign markets, particularly in the so-called developing countries. Certain overseas economies are booming, believe me.

"Anyway," he went on, "when Ray mentioned that all he needed to get his plan off the ground was some financial backing, Harstad expressed an interest. It seems he has some extra capital to invest and thinks that Ray's on to a good thing."

"I'm sorry," said Ashley, "but I don't see where you fit into all this."

"I'm getting to that," said Tyler, giving her a warm smile that lit up his eyes. "Ray, Harstad, and I have formed a partnership to enter into a joint venture with an overseas fish wholesaler. Harstad will put up the cash and will continue to do business with Eagle Island. Most of what we process here will be sold to the wholesaler for overseas distribution. There's just one hitch."

"What's that?"

"As part of the deal," said Tyler, "the foreign wholesaler, who's still very new at this business, is requesting that Ray send a representative to their overseas office to help manage the operation. That's what Ray asked me to do a couple of months ago."

"He wanted you to be his overseas representative?" said Ashley.

"That's right," said Tyler. He gave a gust of laughter at the memory. "At the time, I wasn't even remotely interested, and I told him so."

Then his expression sobered, but the joy remained in his eyes, like twin beacons of light. He leaned toward Ashley.

"But I've changed my mind," he said softly, reaching out to cradle her cheek in his warm hand. "Yesterday, I went looking for Ray to ask him—beg him, if I had to—to take me on as his rep." He gave a meaningful pause.

"You see, I've fallen in love with a woman who's about to relocate to China, and I've promised myself not to let her slip through my fingers."

"Tyler," said Ashley, her heart suddenly thudding in her chest. "Where exactly is this overseas wholesale company?"

"I'll give you three guesses," said Tyler, drawing her toward him, "and two of them don't count."

"Shanghai?" she whispered, hardly daring to believe it.

"That's right, my darling," he said. "China's economy is expanding at an incredible rate and we're going to be part of it." He chuckled deep in his throat. "Are you surprised by my news?"

"I'm—I'm speechless," she said.

"I told you that I'd follow you to China, if I had to," said Tyler, gazing into her eyes with unabashed adoration. "Now do you believe me?"

"Yes," said Ashley, a lump of joyful emotion rising in her throat, "but I never imagined that you would actually find a way to do it."

"Well, imagine it, my love," said Tyler, "because, come fall, you and Elf and I are flying to Shanghai together."

"But who'll run Eagle Island while you're gone?" asked Ashley.

"Bob and Josephine can do it," said Tyler. "I trust them completely. Oh," he added, "I almost forgot. Ray gave me the address for the American School in Shanghai. I need to send for an application to enroll Elf. I think she'll enjoy going to school with embassy kids and the children of business people from all over the world." He grinned. "Speaking of Elf, while we're over there, we'll have to plan a visit to Sichuan Province."

"Sichuan Province?" said Ashley, her head spinning.

"That's right," said Tyler. "Some of the best dinosaur bones in the world have been discovered in that part of China. There's a great museum at a place called—" He pulled a slip of paper from his shirt pocket and read from it. "—a place called Beibei. Elf will love it."

"How do you know all this?" said Ashley.

"Oh," said Tyler, with an airy gesture of his hand, "I did a little research while I was in Kodiak."

"Research?"

"I stopped in at the Kodiak library," he said, "and dug out some information. Since I'll be spending a couple of years in China, I want to learn a few things about the country before I go.

"Say," he added, "that reminds me. I hope you'll start teaching Elf and me a few words of Chinese."

"Tyler, stop," said Ashley with a tremulous laugh. "You're going too fast for me."

"Yes," he said, chuckling along with her, "I guess this is all a bit sudden, isn't it?"

"That's putting it mildly," said Ashley, who could hardly believe the wonderful things that Tyler was telling her. "You seem really excited about going to China."

"You don't know the half of it," he said softly, a look of love smoldering in his eyes. "Speaking of which," he added, "there's just one little detail that we need to clear up."

"What's that?"

There was a soulful pause as Tyler caressed Ashley's cheek and gazed adoringly at her.

"After dinner tonight," he said, "I opened the safe in my office to get this." He reached into his pocket and pulled out a small velvet-covered box. "I want to make you an offer," he said, his features glowing with ardor.

Ashley laughed softly, her voice laced with the love that was spilling from her heart in wave after wave.

"Dear Tyler," she said, gently teasing, but with a tremulous smile up at him, "you make it sound as if you're offering me a contract."

With hands that shook with excitement, she accepted the little box from him.

"You could call it that," he said, a smile spreading across his face. "It's a contract for life, Ashley." He kissed her tenderly. "You know," he said in an aside, "I was very touched when I saw how much trouble you'd gone to for my sake tonight. Why, I think you love this island as much as I do." He kissed her again. "After China, this will all be here waiting for us."

"I do love it here, Tyler," she said with feeling.

"Will you marry me, darling?" he whispered against her lips. "Will you? I love you so much," he said in a voice that was hoarse with yearning. He crushed her to him and murmured against her hair. "Please make me the happiest man in the world and say you'll be my wife. Elf loves you, too." He hugged her tightly. "Sweet Ashley, let's be a family."

"Oh, Tyler," said Ashley, her joy bubbling forth and wreathing her face in smiles. "Of course I'll marry you," she said. "Tyler, I love you more than I can ever say."

"Open the box," he urged, his eyes alight with love and laughter and joy.

She did so and found that it held a beautiful diamond engagement ring.

"It was my mother's," said Tyler, slipping it onto her finger. "If you don't like it, we'll fly to Kodiak and get you a different one."

"No, it's beautiful," said Ashley, admiring the way the faceted gemstone caught the light and sparkled on her finger. "I'd be honored to wear a ring that once belonged to your mother." She looked up at Tyler. "I'm very touched that you'd give it to me."

"I'm glad you like it."

"I can't believe this is happening," said Ashley, through tears of joy. Her fondest dreams were coming true.

"Believe it, sweet Ashley," said Tyler, his deep voice thrumming against her ears. "Believe it for the rest of your life."

Cupping her chin in his hand, he raised her face to his and kissed her with a fervor that snatched her breath away. Then, with the easy confidence of a man who's just won life's greatest prize, he gathered her into his arms. His adoring eyes gazed upon his love. With a sigh of deepest longing, Ashley laced her fingers through Tyler's hair and leaned forward to claim his kisses, her own prize. After several delicious minutes of kissing and hugging, Tyler spoke.

"You didn't fire up the sauna while I was gone, did you?" he said.

"I said I'd wait for you," she gently reminded him, trailing her fingers in a loving caress along his jawline.

"Let's go up there tomorrow," he said, kissing her fingertips, "and fire it up together."

"Time to put past hurts behind you?" she murmured softly.

"Correction," he said, pressing his lips to the palm of her hand. "It's time we *both* put all hurts behind us. From now on, my love, we are going to go forward and leave the past where it belongs—in the past." He paused to drink in her features. "I swear to you," he said, his voice husky with emotion, "to spend the rest of my life making sure that you're never hurt again."

With that sacred vow, he gathered her in his arms once more.

Overflowing with a sense of joy and wonder, Ashley felt her happiness soar as high as the eagles that nested on the island. Tyler's love had healed her heart.